SWORDS OF WIZARDRY
BOOK TWO OF THE SHAMAN'S SWORD SERIES

Robert Ryan

Copyright © 2022 Robert J. Ryan
All Rights Reserved. The right of Robert J. Ryan to be identified as the author of this work has been asserted. All of the characters in this book are fictitious and any resemblance to actual persons, living or dead, is coincidental.

Cover design by www.damonza.com

ISBN: 9798840355602
(print edition)

Trotting Fox Press

Contents

1. He Will Come — 3
2. Let Me Help — 12
3. The Eyes of the Shamans — 20
4. The Noose Tightens — 30
5. All Ways are Dangerous — 36
6. The Seer — 41
7. Remember Me — 51
8. The Woman in Black — 60
9. Always Silent — 70
10. Betrayal — 76
11. Deeper into the Mists — 84
12. The Black Fox — 94
13. A Sign of Luck — 100
14. Rumor — 108
15. The Oath Stone — 115
16. A Difficult Choice — 121
17. Parley — 128
18. The Emperor Returns! — 135
19. Battle and Blood — 140
20. The Night Walker Clan — 148
21. A Swift Knife — 154
22. On Bended Knee — 160
23. Then Kill Me — 165
24. Judge My Character — 170
25. Celebration — 175
26. Cold Steel — 183
Appendix: Encyclopedic Glossary — 194

1. He Will Come

Drasta Gan sat alone in his hut, and he felt the burden of his long years, steeped in evil, weigh heavily upon him. But he shrugged. Good and evil were nothing but words.

He did not have the secret of longevity, that highest of magics, which some of his brethren did. Life was precious therefore, and the joy of it must be seized. The strong prospered and the weak fell by the wayside. That was the rule of nature, and he abided by it. He would not change now, and he knew that his misgivings would pass. Even so, when he had seen the light on the western horizon it had shocked him and brought the shadow of fear to his heart.

He had been awoken by a clamor outside, and he sent the young witches that served him out of his hut to discover what was going on. When one of them returned to tell him, he could make nothing of her babbling.

Yet the instant he had gone out himself, he had understood. The great blaze of light on the western horizon was brighter than the growing dawn of the east. It could mean only one thing, and it was the thing all shamans for a thousand years had told themselves would never happen, yet they feared it anyway.

The heir to the emperor had come forth, and they had found the twin swords of their ancestor. It spelled chaos for the land, and all that the shamans had worked for was at risk. Nothing would ever be the same again.

A long while he had gazed at that light, and it was only when the full rising of the sun extinguished it that he had returned inside his hut, sending the witches to scatter out of his way with a curse.

He needed to be alone, and to think this through. Only he, the shaman of the Two Ravens Clan, knew what it meant, and when he decided what to do about it, then, and then alone, would he tell the rest.

Yet first, he needed confirmation and whatever other news there was. For that, he must consult with another shaman, and one closer to the center of things. That vexed him. He did not like it here in this backwater land of hills and mists among a barbaric tribe. He had been born to greater things, but always luck had eluded him. He must now speak to one of his betters, no matter that it should have been him in the position of greater authority.

Drasta calmed himself. Such thoughts were not conducive to summoning magic. A tranquil mind was needed instead.

He sat down on the chair before the crude hearth in the hut. It was nothing more than a circle of stones on the earthen floor, and the room reeked of smoke from the fitful flames. Not all of it escaped through the small hole in the peaked roof. Once more he felt his anger at the world rise to the surface, but he suppressed it.

Taking deep breaths, he slowly drew his mind into a pattern of tranquility. He concentrated on the dancing flames, and he watched how they leaped and twisted before they disappeared, yet new ones took their place in an endless succession.

The hut faded from his mind. There were only the flames. Them, and his magic. He felt it stir like a living being inside him, somehow separate from him, with its own life, yet part of him too.

He offered up a prayer in the old tongue of the shamans, and he felt the magic blossom to life. Over a vast distance his spell reached, spanning the numberless miles between himself and the Nagrak shaman that he sought communion with.

For some moments nothing happened, then a face flared to life within the flames. It was Drugu, a man he hated yet also feared. Once they had been rivals, but now Drasta must bend the knee to him. Through good luck Drugu had found escaped prisoners and been rewarded by the shaman elders with greater power and knowledge of the longevity magic. It was also rumored that he had used an assassin to remove a shaman who stood in the way of his advancement.

Drasta bowed. "Greetings, brother."

"Be quick," Drugu replied. "I'm busy."

Anger flared in Drasta, but he kept his head lowered and did not show it.

"Is it true? Have the twin swords been found?"

"Don't bother me with stupid questions. You must have seen the magic, otherwise you would not have contacted me."

Again Drasta hid his boiling anger. "Who is the heir and have they been found yet?"

"It is a girl. Her name is Shar, and she is from the Fen Wolf tribe."

Drasta noticed that no answer had been given as to whether or not she had been found. He knew that meant no, but it would be wise to ignore the omission.

"This is the same Shar then that we were warned to keep watch for? The one who was outlawed and could be killed?"

"The very same," Drugu said impatiently. "If you see her, kill her on sight. There's no reason for her to go to your hills though. There's nothing there for her. We expect her to return to Tsarin Fen. It's the only place she has a chance of raising an army. So, against that possibility, send your nazram to meet with others on the western border."

Drasta bowed again. "It will be done."

The spell faded then, and there was nothing left to say anyway. For all the efforts of the shamans over a vast stretch of time, the prophecy had been fulfilled and they faced a great threat once again. It was a sobering thought.

Worse, despite Drugu's mask of power and control, there was a bubbling well of uncertainty underneath. That made Drasta smile though, for he did not like Drugu at all and reveled in his discomfort. Greater power held greater responsibility, and as he was the closest senior shaman to where the swords had been hidden the expectation of finding and killing the heir would fall to him, as would the price of failure.

The smile faded from his face. This was a time of change, and all things were possible. Destiny was in the air, and he could almost smell the prophecy. His instincts were aroused, and regardless of what these events meant for the land, he must discover what might occur in his own small territory. He did not like the mist-shrouded hills that served as home, but they were all he had at the moment and he would protect them.

He knew what he must do next. He did not have the longevity magic. He was not a senior shaman, but that did not mean he did not have power.

Few, or none, of the shamans had his skill with divination. He must consult the dead and learn from them the truth of what might happen in his hills. It was not something that he looked forward to though.

Raising the spirits of the dead was dangerous, and that was why few shamans ever learned the lore, or if they did, why they did not practice it. But his father had taught him, as his father had learned from his own before, stretching back through a long line to the time of the emperor himself.

He built up the fire. He would have great need of its warmth, and its light also. Then he drew off the necklace he wore and placed it on the dirt floor. It was a grim thing, for the teeth of the enemies he had killed were strung upon it, and it was gruesome to look upon. That made it valuable too, for it cowed most of the superstitious hill men that he mostly dealt with. They feared one of their own teeth being collected for it. As well they should.

The teeth served another purpose. They were a link to the dead, and it was fitting to summon enemies and compel from them their knowledge of the future rather than to trouble the rest of friends.

Drasta breathed deep and found tranquility again, and then he chanted once more. It was a prayer to Harledrek, the snake-headed goddess of death. Even as he prayed he sensed his magic flare to life once more, but this spell was different from the last.

Another magic rose in response. It came from deep in the earth, and it swirled up like tendrils of a vine seeking something on which to climb. He shuddered when it touched him, but he accepted that embrace. To speak to the dead, he must draw close to death himself.

Cold filled the hut. It was a numbing cold that seeped into bones and made him tremble. It was the touch of death itself, and it turned moisture in the air into frost that settled over anything metal.

The fire burned brightly, but the warmth of it seemed as nothing. Then it popped and flared before dimming as though there were no air in the room.

Darkness filled the hut then, and the fire seemed nothing more than a spark. And in the dark was something worse than cold. It contained all the spirits of his dead enemies. He saw them here and there, if only a gleam of ghostly eyes or a pallid cheek. He saw them, and it troubled him. It was normal for the goddess to send several spirits, but *all* of them was something he had never experienced nor heard tell of.

"Obey me," he commanded, as the spell required.

"We obey," came the hiss of a reply from a corner of the room, but the other spirits remained silent.

Drasta ordered his thoughts. "The swords of Dawn and Dusk have been discovered. This will bring chaos to the land. Is it not so?"

From a different corner another whisper came in answer.

"The land is *always* in chaos. This is the nature of humanity. Yet for a while it will increase."

Drasta gritted his teeth. It was always like this when speaking to the dead. It was a barrier that nature did not wish broken, and the answers that came across that great divide were in riddles and half-truths.

"Chaos," he said, "rules the land of the Cheng and all others. Yet what of these hills in which I live? What troubles will come here?"

The spirits moved to and fro in the shadows, but no reply came.

"Answer me!" Drasta commanded. "The spell binds you."

There was a noise in the shadows that might have been laughter, and it sent a chill up Drasta's spine. Had he cast the spell with some error? Or were there just too many spirits for him to control?

A voice whispered from above him. "Many troubles will come. All over the land the old rules began to fray. They will either break or be bound tighter still. Yet to this place one comes in particular that you will fear above all others."

Drasta did not look up. This was the way of spirits, to try to put fear into those who summoned them by tricks and deceit. He looked steadily into the dim flame that remained, and thought. Who was it that he feared most?

It did not take him long to arrive at an answer, and it was in truth the greatest threat to the order of the Two Ravens Tribe that he had established.

"Kubodin will return," he whispered, and realized that there had been fear in his voice.

The spirits laughed again in the dark, and Drasta felt anger bubble to the surface.

"Answer me!" he commanded again. "Kubodin will return. Is that not so?"

"Yes," came a voice from behind him. "You have named your greatest fear, and the knowledge of the dead confirms it. Kubodin comes, and he seeks to overthrow the chief that you set in his place by your schemes."

It was a revelation, for Kubodin had escaped the death set for him a long time ago, and Drasta had long since put the matter aside. It was a mistake. He should have hired Ahat to find and kill him.

"Will he succeed in claiming the chieftainship?"

There was a rustle in the shadows, and another spirit answered haughtily.

"Fate is not set. This you know without asking us. Some things are likely to occur, and others are less so. Kubodin will come, but neither his success nor yours is yet certain." The voice trailed away, and Drasta was thinking of another question when the spirit spoke again, this time in a rising voice.

"We see him coming! Already his steps are turning this way. Like the surging of the sea he comes against you, and if you do not stop him he will destroy all in his path, and leave you, and the chieftain who rules in his stead, in utter ruin."

Drasta began to ask more, but the spirits spoke now in one voice, and it was as thunder in his ears.

"You have been warned! We will say no more, for your spell is at an end. Let us rest in peace now, and call us not again for seven moons. You know the lore. Before then you will be triumphant. Or dead."

A great wind blew then, and it seemed as though the hut would blow over, yet it remained as it was. All that changed was that the darkness and cold faded away, and the flames of the fire burned hotly again.

Drasta knelt down before it, as close as he could get. The cold had seeped into his bones and his breath was a billowing mist.

For a long while he stayed thus, shivering and wretched before the fire. Slowly though he felt warmth seep back into him, and the racing of his heart stopped hammering into his ribs.

It had been a strange summoning, and unlike any that he had done before. He supposed that was because of the times. It was a triseptium year, and prophecy and chaos swept over the land like a storm, and even the dead felt it.

He wished he had been able to ask more questions, but he had learned what he needed. He had even learned whence Kubodin would come, though the spirits had tried to conceal that.

Like the surging of the sea he comes, they had warned. They had not wanted to say that he would enter the hills by the fishing village in the north that served as the entry point to the land, but he had discerned their riddle easily and they had not been able to keep the truth from him.

It was troubling, for that was not in Two Ravens Clan territory. More troubling was a nagging feeling that although he had compelled them to tell the truth, he had not had the chance to ask all the questions he wished. He might have missed something that would have bearing on his decisions. But he knew enough.

Kubodin must be killed quickly. And the nazram could travel over all lands. Despite what he had said to Drugu, he would not send them to Tsarin Fen. He would send them to the fishing village so they could waylay Kubodin. He must die before he had a chance to stir up rebellion.

2. Let Me Help

Shar stood still and waited. She had asked for the help of these men, and she had admitted to them the truth. Being the emperor's heir was nothing by itself. She could only achieve something if she united the sundered tribes.

"I'll do as you ask," one of the men said. He too had been a quester for the swords, but he drew off the white armband that signified it, and cast it away. "The swords are not for me, but I can still help. I'll spread the word about you wherever I go."

Shar nodded gravely to him. "There will be danger in that. Avoid the shamans, for they will silence you if they can."

The remaining two questers agreed as well, as did the witnesses they had brought with them. Then they departed. But one of the questers held back, seemingly in an intense discussion with his friends, then they left, yet he approached Shar.

"Let me help you," he said.

Shar studied him. He seemed little older than a boy, but there was a hard glint in his eyes that said his short life had not been easy. She did not trust him though. Only moments ago he himself had been seeking the swords. Would he so easily give up the desire for them? Did he believe the legend that only the true heir could touch them, and anyone else would be struck down by their magic?

"I thank you for your offer. But I'll be pursued now, by nazram and by dark sorcery. It's better for you to be well away from me."

He grinned at her, and he seemed even younger but the smile did not soften his eyes.

"Without doubt, I'd be safer elsewhere. But that's not the point. I can help you. I'm a fine warrior, and a good tracker. You'll need both those skills to survive."

Behind her, the great magic that lit the sky with a ruddy light was fading as the full light of day spread across the land. Shar knew she was running out of time and had to leave swiftly.

"Again, I thank you. I have with me two skilled warriors. One of them is Asana. And I'm a fair tracker myself."

She saw the cool gaze of the young man briefly light on Asana and scrutinize him, but it shifted back to her swiftly.

"I'm a better warrior than you may think, and three can help you more than two. But I offer another, and more needed skill as well."

He pointed back toward the Fields of Rah. "That way lies death. It's a populous land, and there are shamans and nazram aplenty. Your enemies will soon find you, and kill you." He took a step forward then, and swept his arm up to point to the forested ridges that lay behind Chatchek Fortress. "But in that direction is a vast wilderness. It's high country, and remote. There, you can slip away from your enemies, and I can help you. I know those lands well."

Shar thought hard and swiftly. She did not want help from another quester, for she had no reason to trust any of them. Yet what this man said was true. Already she had decided that those remote-looking ridges were her best chance of evading pursuit. And if this man knew them like he claimed, that might be the difference between life and death.

Could she trust him though? She did not give trust easily, and for that there was good reason. Yet he was little more than a boy, and she just could not see how there could be darkness in his soul.

She made her decision. "Very well, lead us up into the ridges. But you must know first that to go with me is to court your own death. My enemies are powerful, and if they find me they'll kill you too. Do you still wish to come?"

The young man looked at her with those eyes that were older than his years, and shrugged.

"I do what I do for my people, and death might strike me down ploughing a field. I'll take my chances with you."

He said nothing more, and strode ahead of them toward the ridges. Shar looked at Asana and Kubodin. They had offered no advice, but she read doubt in their glances. If the young man knew the land ahead as he claimed though, his help would be invaluable. If not, she could still send him away.

They followed him, and Shar called out. "What's your name, lad?"

"Nerchak," he replied, but he kept striding ahead as though he feared she might change her mind if she had more time to talk to him.

They moved quickly despite the steep upward slope. Chatchek Fortress soon fell away behind them, and in the full daylight that now bathed it, and from this angle, it looked much more decrepit than it had last night. Terrible things had happened there, and a great one too. She glanced back for a final look as they climbed one of the ridges thickly grown with trees, and her hand strayed to the hilts of her twin swords.

Nerchak led them deep into the trees, and he seemed to find animal trails swiftly and the quickest and easiest way forward despite the thick growth.

Shar looked at the trees, and they were unlike any she was used to. She was in a different world now, and all that she knew and had done was of less use. That meant, more and more, she would have to rely on others. One could not become emperor without it. Or in her present circumstances, even survive.

It was her nature though to be a loner. It did not come easily to her to accept help or advice. At times, that would be a strength. At other times it would be a weakness, and she must practice evaluating a situation to decide which way was the best one forward.

Her doubts of Nerchak were fading though. He had not lied, for he was skilled at woodcraft and found, wherever possible, ways to hide their trail. So too he really did seem to know this place.

All morning they climbed higher, ascending from one ridge to another. The woods were often thick, but so much different from what she knew. In the fen, the trees were usually stunted and there was much undergrowth. Here though, the trees seemed like giants, yet under them it was often bare of growth and just a deep blanket of leaf litter slowly turning to rich soil.

At times the ridges were bare, and though Nerchak avoided such places wherever he could, it was not always possible. Shar loved them though, despite the risk of being seen. Every time they came to one, they would pause and look back over the lower ridges below and far out over the green smudge that was the Fields of Rah.

There was nothing like this sense of height and distant views in Tsarin Fen. Shar loved the beauty of it, yet it served a practical purpose too. If there were enemies out there looking for her, this would give her a chance of seeing them.

They saw nothing out of place though. Perhaps their choice of direction had confounded the enemy. Or maybe after all these years the enemy had been ill-prepared and caught by surprise. Whatever the case, this little bit of good luck would not last. It must be taken advantage of.

They stopped seldom for any rests, and when they did it was not for long. Shar was impatient to move ahead, and Nerchak sensed her will to do so, or had his own desire to do so, and led them exactly as she would have led them through the swampland that she knew: swiftly, silently and as near to invisibly as was possible.

Sometime after noon the land began to change. They no longer climbed but instead traversed a plateau. It was still rugged going, for though it was not uphill anymore the countryside was crisscrossed by many swiftly running streams and between them there were still ridges, if only small compared to what had gone before. There were less trees too, and the ground was rocky in places.

Nerchak used both to good effect. Often he took the travelers through streams, walking along them for some distance before going up on the opposite bank in order to slow down any tracker who pursued them. Likewise, he used the rocky ground to hide their trail and change direction.

This was not all he did. At times he even had them climb trees where they grew very thickly and move from branch to branch for a little distance so as to leave no trail, and where he could he did this to get them into a stream which he used to obscure their passage completely.

Shar began to respect his abilities. He had done little that the rest of them would not have thought of, but he had done it with speed. Part of this was his own high skill, and part of it stemmed from a good knowledge of this country. He had not lied about that at all, and he was proving to be an asset.

She could not help but wonder how someone so young had acquired such skill. She was glad he possessed it though.

The long day passed, and Shar knew without doubt that the enemy had at the very least reached Chatchek Fortress. The speed at which Nerchak traveled was the very thing that gave the travelers their one and only advantage. The deeper they went into this rugged land, and the greater the lead they had, the more opportunity they had to hide their trail. Best of all, it provided for the chance that it might rain. If that happened, whatever small trail they left would be obliterated before they could be found.

Long shadows signaled that the day was drawing to a close, and high up as they were the temperature fell quickly too.

"There are caves close by," Nerchak informed them, and he changed direction a little heading up toward a slight ridge.

Shar followed doggedly. She was tired, but she tried not to show it. Neither Asana nor Kubodin did either, but she knew that they would feel it just as she did. Yet Nerchak strode up the slope as though he were just starting a journey.

The caves were well hidden. There were several openings in a shear rock face, but the entrances were small and not visible unless someone came very close. That, Shar hoped, would not happen. But if it did, the small opening would serve the purpose of providing a good defensive spot.

Another thought occurred to her though. "Are these caves connected inside?"

Nerchak grinned at her. "No. Have no fear, if the worst comes to the worst, we need only defend one entrance."

It was the answer she hoped to hear, but once again the young man surprised her. He was not just a skilled woodsman, but he also understood warrior strategy.

They made camp in one of the caves, and it was a dark and dingy place. Yet they had access to firewood, and this they gathered and used to build a small fire at the back of the cave. The place would soon reek of smoke because there was nowhere for it to escape from, but that was of no concern. They would have heat and light, and the fire would not reveal them to anyone who was searching the area. If the enemy came this way at all.

They sat around the fire and ate a larger meal than usual, for they had worked hard through the day. It was difficult terrain, and they had covered many, many miles.

When they were done though, Shar broached the subject that had been on her mind all day.

"This high country is a good place to hide, but we can't stay here forever. Where do you think I should go next?"

Asana put a small branch on the fire. "Your life is in peril wherever you go. You need help. More than we can give you."

"I know. I need an army."

Kubodin fingered his brass earring, which Shar had learned meant that he was thinking hard about something.

"Asana is right. Come to the Wahlum Hills, where I'm from and where my tribe still lives. It's remote, and the enemy are less likely to seek you there than in other places. And if I gain control of the tribe as I have a mind to do, I'll be able to help you."

Shar considered that, but she was not so sure. She would need an army, and even if Kubodin was successful, the support of a small hill tribe would not help her much. At the same time though, the shamans knew that she must raise an army, and the larger tribes would all be watched more closely.

"Before you make up your mind, know this," Asana told her. "We'll go with you wherever you want, but when Shulu spoke to Kubodin and I, she indicated that Kubodin will return to his homeland."

Shar was not ready to make a decision. Instead, she excused herself and went out of the cave mouth and gazed at the lands lower down through which they had climbed. What she saw surprised her.

The lower ground surrounding where Chatchek Fortress must stand was alight with the campfires of the enemy. There must be an army there, and all looking for her.

3. The Eyes of the Shamans

Shar gazed out at the campfires of the enemy, and they were like the stars in the sky. For a moment, she felt as though all the world was against her. She could not overcome such a determined opposition. The shamans would find her. Torture her. And kill her.

Tears welled in her eyes, and for the first time she truly appreciated the immensity of her task. It was impossible. Despite her ancestor, she was an ordinary person. The swords were not enough. Ten thousand swords, and warriors to wield them, would not be enough. Despair crushed her, and she felt a flood of tears welling up.

She dashed them away with a sob. Then she straightened. If nothing else, she could at least face her fate bravely. She might be beaten, but her spirit would never be defeated.

A cool breeze touched the tear-wetted skin of her face, and she pushed down the dark thoughts that had nearly swamped her. Maybe she would die. And certainly she was no one special. Only the blood in her veins was different, but that counted for nothing unless she lived up to it.

Somewhere in the dark down there the fortress hulked, and she remembered the feeling she had experienced as she stood before it, in the same place that her great ancestor had once stood. It was a moment shared between them despite the vast gulf of time that kept them apart.

But it was not the only experience they shared. Did not Chen Fei himself start life as an ordinary person? Yet step by step he made something of himself. Did he not face the exact same threat that she did now? A sea of enemies against him and the dark might of the shamans? Yet in the end he beat them back and united the Cheng into one great empire that prospered.

He had done it. He had done it all. Perhaps she would always live in his shadow. Perhaps she would fail. Or not. His blood *did* run in her veins, and she would emulate him if she could. And if not, then death was not to be feared. He had been there before her too, and he had died well.

The breeze ruffled her hair, and she tilted her chin upward. Then possessed by some wild instinct she drew the swords of Dawn and Dusk and lifted them above her head, the blades crossing.

"Do you hear me, O shamans? I'm coming for you! The journey will be long, but I will bring you low and free this land, or die trying. I swear it! Fear me, for I come!"

The swords felt good in her hands, and she sensed something of the magic that was in them. The shamans might not have heard her, but the demon entrapped in the blades had. She felt from it a hint of emotion. It might have been anticipation. It certainly was not laughter.

She sheathed the blades and then spun around. Some instinct had warned her, and sure enough Asana was there, paused halfway through exiting the cave mouth.

"I'm sorry," the swordmaster said. "I didn't mean to overhear that. I merely came out to check on you."

It was not his fault. "You could hardly be expected to know that I was going to talk to myself."

He grinned at that, but said nothing as he came over to join her. Together, they looked out over the sea of campfires.

"Does it scare you?" he asked softly after some time.

It was not what she had expected him to say. If anything, she would have thought he would have told her that all would be well and that they had a plan to escape.

Most men would have ignored the problem and gone straight to the solution.

"It *does* scare me."

"I'm not surprised. It scares me too, and I'm not one prone to doubt or fear. Your enemy is great. There's no shame in fearing the forces they can send against you. Nor is there wisdom in ignoring it. Only a fool would try to do so."

They were silent again for some while. The breeze stirred Shar's hair once more, and a tiny bat, or several in succession, flitted around them in the dark and then disappeared.

"Do you know what I fear most of all?" she asked.

"Tell me."

"I fear my destiny. What if I succeed? I will bring war and chaos to the land. Blood will run in rivers."

Asana sighed. "I don't blame you. Fate has wedged you into a corner, and there's no good way out. Fight, and things will come to pass as you suggest. Give up, and you will die, and the chance of freedom for the Cheng will die with you. The shamans will rule as they always have, and tribe will fight tribe and blood will still be spilled."

Far away the campfires were starting to burn less brightly. The soldiers had finished their meals and needed them no more. They would probably keep burning for hours though.

Asana turned to face her. "Whatever happens, you won't face it alone. You have friends, and we'll help you. And I don't doubt you'll meet more along the way."

She hoped that was true. She would need an army of them.

They lingered a little while longer, watching the distant fires that looked so pretty yet brought terror to Shar's heart, and then they went back inside the cave.

The smell of smoke was strong, and it stung Shar's eyes. It would soon fade away though, for the fire was already burning low.

"Well," Nerchak asked. "Where will we head tomorrow?"

Shar sat down by the dying fire. "To the Wahlum Hills, and Kubodin's tribe."

The young man pursed his lips. "Have you considered staying here? I can hide you here for months and then we can go back to more populous lands when the hunt for you has died away."

"I've considered all options, including that. But it seems Shulu intended me to go with Kubodin, so I'll walk that trail and see where it takes me."

Nerchak gave a shrug. For all that he was young he was good at hiding his emotions, but she sensed that it was not the decision he would have taken. When he spoke again though, he did not try to dissuade her.

"Is Shulu really still alive? What is she like?"

Shar did not really want to talk about the subject. She was very private, but this young man was risking his life to help her.

"She's very much alive, and she's much as you'd expect. She has an aura of power about her. She's the greatest of all the shamans that have ever lived, and she knows it. And yet, to me, she was like a kindly grandmother."

That seemed to satisfy Nerchak. Or else he was perceptive enough to realize that it was a topic she did not really wish to keep talking about.

She decided to change the subject back to what they were talking about before he had a chance to change his mind.

"The Wahlum Hills it is for us. For me, it's become emperor or die. And something about going with

Kubodin feels right. It's a remote place, and the enemy will have a harder time discovering me there. And if they do, it'll take longer for them to send an army that far. That gives me more time to try to build my own."

She glanced at Kubodin. He too sat by the fire, and he cradled his axe in his lap, running his fingers gently over the sharp edge of it blades. He looked determined about something, but she was not sure what.

"What do you think, Kubodin?" she asked. "There are quite a few tribes in those hills of yours, if I learned my lessons well from my grandmother. Do you think I can sway some of the chiefs to support me?"

He grinned at her. "You could persuade a thirsty man to toss his waterbag away. Still, the hill tribes are independent. Or at least they seem so compared to the rest of the Cheng. The shamans still rule there, as everywhere else, but they have to talk fast to get their way. They'll demand your death, and the chiefs will hand you over quickly. Unless you can convince them not to. That won't be easy, but I think they'll at least listen to you. Afterward, who can say? They're independent, but they're also unpredictable."

That was also what her grandmother had told her about the hill tribes, and Shar believed it. Kubodin himself seemed the perfect representation of what they were said to be like. That was no bad thing though. Wild and rough he might be. Quick to anger, slow to forget a grudge and fast to pick a fight with someone he did not like, maybe. Yet he was also a fine warrior, tough as the hills from which he came and loyal to death. A small army of men like him could conquer the world.

Her decision was made, and it was time to sleep. They set no watch, for they feared no discovery. Not yet, anyway. Tomorrow would be another day and she would see what skills and resources the enemy had.

If they found her, then it would be a race to escape and a good night's sleep would serve them well. She was bitterly tired, and sleep came swift and deep.

If Shar dreamed, or woke during the night, she did not remember it. When the light of dawn seeped in through the cave mouth she was awake and refreshed. Breakfast was a quick business, and they left the cave even as the sun was rising a hand's span above the rim of the world.

They waited a moment at the mouth of the cave, listening and watching for any sign of the enemy. There was nothing.

"Veer a little to the east today," Kubodin told Nerchak. "That will take us to the Wahlum Hills."

The young man nodded and obliged. He led them in that direction, setting the same fast pace he had yesterday. Speed was important because none of them believed that their trail at the fortress had not been found. What must be hoped for though was that at some point the enemy would lose it. That was where speed came in handy. The more time they had, the more they could hide their trail by trick and deception. Each time they did that successfully they might slow any pursuit by hours. And a point would come where they would lose the trail completely.

Rain would help that. Shar glanced skyward, but there were few clouds and no indication the weather would change any time soon.

They plodded on, resting infrequently and for short periods. The countryside remained much as it had yesterday, though perhaps the trees grew even more thickly. That was a good thing, helping hide them from view. Yet it also meant that at those times when they rested and studied their backtrail, they could see little of it and could not be sure if the enemy was not there and gaining on them.

Once more Nerchak led them well, and he really did seem to know these lands intimately. That was a great advantage, not least because he headed for places where he could work to hide all sign of their passage.

It was not long before they came across such a place, and his skill was put to good use. It was a gorge of sorts, where a river must have run in the ancient past, yet now it was dry and the steep sides and bottom were of rock.

There were rock pools in places with good water, but he avoided these. The stone near them was more cracked and there was mud and sand that might leave a trail.

He navigated the gorge for hundreds of feet, but at length found what he was looking for. A tree grew up from a crack in the rock, and it reached up high. High enough, in fact, that its taller branches spread out over the banks above.

"We'll climb out here," he said. "Try to leave no mark on the bark."

Shar went first, and she enjoyed it. She was good at climbing trees, and though this was taller than she was used to she scampered up it swiftly and then jumped onto the ground beyond the bank of the gorge.

Luck favored them here too. It was heavily forested on this side of the gorge, and the leaf mold was thick. When they were done they could use a branch to hide their trail.

The others came up after her, only Kubodin having any trouble. Mostly because his axe was cumbersome and the blades caught on twigs and branches.

Nerchak came up last, and there was a boyish grin on his face.

"If they manage to follow us this far, that should throw them off the trail."

Shar felt his enthusiasm. She was skilled at tracking and hiding a trail, but this land was different from what she was used to. Even so, she knew that only the best of the best could follow them through all the deceptions that Nerchak had used. She was grateful to have him, and she knew beyond doubt that his skill had made a massive difference. Without him, they might all be dead already.

They continued on. Surprisingly, they came to what seemed to be an ancient road. It was mostly overgrown by trees, but here and there Shar saw the signs of an advanced design.

There was nothing like this in Tsarin Fen, but Shulu had described the way these roads were built. They had a slight curve to them, shedding water to each side to help drain it and make it passable in poor weather. And on the higher side there was a drainage ditch to divert water that would otherwise flow across it from the lands above.

"Where there's a road there are people," Asana commented.

"Not here," Nerchak replied. "Although there once were. You'll see."

They went ahead, and in a short time they did see. The road led to a ruined city. Shar had never seen a city before, and the thought of so many people living so close together was strange to her. It did not seem natural, but it was what it was, and she understood the benefits too.

She looked around as they entered through a broken archway. There were no walls here. This place could never be defended properly. But it was also old. If Chatchek Fortress had been old, this was older by far. There was virtually nothing left, and it seemed little more than a mound of earth out of which rose the last remnants of a civilization that must have predated the Cheng.

"I've heard of this place," Kubodin said, looking around with a frown. "Antrathadaba it's called."

Nerchak looked at him sharply. "Few know that name."

"It was the capital of the people who lived here before the Cheng. We have legends of them in my tribe, and more than legends. For in the Wahlum Hills there are ruined cities like this too. From here to there were once their lands."

"That, I didn't know," Nerchak replied.

They climbed the sloping earth that covered the dead city like a burial mound. It was strange to Shar to think that once people had lived here and dreamed the dreams of life. But all were forgotten now. All were dead. They were nothing more than dust and their hopes were as ashes on the wind. All that remained of them was an unusual name, and perhaps the same fate awaited the Cheng one day.

It did not matter to her. All a person could do was live the life they had, and it was the same for a civilization. What came before or after was less important than what they did while they lived. Yet still, it was a sobering thought that even a civilization could die, and it was a reminder to her to be vigilant against such a thing. No doubt an entire people could lose their way and hasten their demise just as a careless person could die of avoidable accident or injury.

They came down off the mound during the afternoon and entered a thick forest again, but it was not as before. Perhaps these lands had once been farms, for now there were many patches of clear ground amid the stands of trees.

In one such clearing Asana gave a warning and ushered them back into the cover of trees.

"What is it?" Shar whispered, her hands on the hilts of her swords.

"Maybe nothing," he replied. "But look up into the sky."

Shar did so. "I see two eagles circling, nothing more."

Kubodin grunted. "Eagles maybe. Or maybe the eyes of the shamans seeking us."

4. The Noose Tightens

The travelers stayed under the cover of the trees. High above, the eagles circled, and Shar thought back to what Shulu had told her of the shamans.

Magic was not a skill that Shar had any affinity for. Even so, Shulu had given her instruction in the matter. Her enemies possessed it, and would use it as a weapon against her. For that reason it had been a key part of her training.

It was certainly possible that the shamans might use sorcery to see through the eyes of a bird, or another animal. It was not a common magic, but it could be done. It could be detected too, but not by Shar. Only another shaman had a chance of doing so.

Though it was possible, it seemed unlikely. Yet she held that thought in check. Who was she to say what was likely or not, as far as the shamans were concerned? They had feared the prophecy for a thousand years. They had hidden the swords, and no doubt they had made preparations against the chance that one such as her would arise.

She had no way to know if the eagles were just eagles, or if the shamans were using them. So the only choice was to remain hidden until they drifted away.

But waiting was a problem. Every moment of delay gave any enemy on foot a greater chance of catching up to them. It irked her, but there was nothing to be done but wait.

She smiled when she looked over at Kubodin though. He had merely laid himself down and used his cloak as a pillow. He might even have gone to sleep.

Asana seemed relaxed but alert. Nerchak squatted down and leaned back against a tree. Of them all, she seemed the most nervous and she did not like it. It was not like her, but it seemed to her that the weight of the world was being lowered onto her shoulders.

Time passed slowly, and at first Shar thought she was imagining it when the long slow circles of the eagles appeared to drift southward, but then it became increasingly obvious that it was so, and not long after they disappeared from sight altogether.

"Well, shamans or no shamans," Kubodin said, "they've gone, and it's best we do the same."

The little man had never been asleep at all, and Shar should have known it. He was always alert no matter that it appeared otherwise.

They took up the journey again, but from then onward they kept a sharp eye at the sky and Nerchak led them as much as possible through dense woods.

Once more, the countryside began to change. It was flatter now, and there were less forests. It was in one of many clearings that they came upon an ancient battlefield. There was little sign of it, and they would never have known except that a stele marked the spot.

They stopped and looked at this, while Kubodin kept watch skyward.

It was a strange stone, tall as a man and as wide on all four of its sides, which were smooth and flat. It had curious writing on it, which Shar could not read, but it had neatly carved scenes of battle as well. Shar was amazed at how lifelike the images were even though they had been etched into stone.

"This is old," Asana said. He pointed to some of the figures. "See how differently the swords are shaped? And the armor? This isn't in the Cheng style. Not now, nor even from the emperor's time. At least not from the old books I've read that had drawings in them."

Shar knew what he meant. The swords were longer and larger, and the images of the men wielding them seemed taller and bigger framed too.

"Can anyone read the writing?" she asked.

No one could, not even Asana who was learned in such things.

"Are there any stories of this place?" Asana asked Nerchak.

"Not that I know of. I've never been to this exact spot before, and I didn't know it was here."

"But you grew up here?"

Nerchak hesitated, then shook his head. "No. No one lives here. At least not now, but I hid here for a while. Anyway, we shouldn't stay long in the open like this."

The young man led them out of the clearing and under cover of the trees again. Who he had been hiding from, no one asked. It was not their business to know unless he told them.

They moved silently and swiftly. Nerchak led, and Shar had taken to following up the rear. It was her task to ensure they were not caught by surprise by any who pursued them and managed to get close without detection. To this end, she often trailed twenty or thirty feet back so that the slight noise they made was less conspicuous and she was better able to hear any noise from behind. Likewise, she often stopped and scanned the backtrail.

It was this habit that saved them. The first thing she noticed was a flight of birds taking off in the distance behind them. It could have been nothing, but she became wary and watched and listened harder.

The minutes passed, and there was nothing. But then she saw a lone bird swooping in to land in a tree suddenly veer to the side.

"Hst!" she warned the others. "Draw your weapons and hide."

She ran ahead the twenty feet that separated them and they moved swiftly into a thick stand of timber. They were lucky, for there was a deep undergrowth of ferns here that gave them excellent concealment.

There they waited in silence. No one asked what she had heard or seen. No one doubted her. They were ready to fight for her, and even lose their lives for her. But she hoped it would not come to that.

The whinny of a horse drifted to them, and it seemed distant. Shar knew better though. Trees muffled sound, and she did not think the rider was far away at all.

She was soon proved correct. Only it was not one rider but a group of six. They emerged out of a patch of trees a hundred feet away, and that was good news. They were not following any tracks, so it might be that they had not found their quarry but were simply on patrol.

The riders drew their mounts to a halt and talked among each other. What they said, Shar could not hear. They were too far away. Yet one lifted his head back and laughed. Some of the others joined in, and then the lead rider seemed to say something and they kicked their mounts forward again.

There was another stand of trees ahead of them, but they veered to the south of it and disappeared from sight. Shar remained still, as did the others. For a while the sound of the riders came back to them as they continued on their way, but then it slowly faded and was gone.

"Just a patrol," Shar whispered.

Asana sheathed his blade. "So it seems. They didn't look like men alert for an enemy. They were just riding through country that someone had designated them to search. They had no idea we were close, otherwise they'd have been more wary."

Shar agreed. But how long then before another patrol, or the next one, or the one after, discovered them by accident?

They waited a little longer, ensuring the riders did not double back or that it was not some kind of trick.

"You made the right choice," Kubodin said softly. "Imagine how many more people would be looking for you if you had gone to more populous lands in the south or west?"

"True. It seems there are enough of the enemy here though."

Kubodin ran a hand through his straggly hair. "Aye. There are a few here, but it'll be better when we reach the Wahlum Hills. At least if we can slip away from here undetected. Then it'll take them quite a while to find you. Better still, they'll probably think you're making for one of the larger tribes, or maybe even back to the Fen Wolves where you'd have support."

That was true. She *would* have support there, and the shamans might well expect her to return home. It was the obvious place to go to start to raise an army, which they knew she must do to live as well as she knew it herself. For that very reason though, she could not go there. They would be expecting it. Yet it might draw their resources away from here.

Her time to return home would come though. When it did, she would have strength and power and an army at her back. She would bring woe and despair to the shaman who had tried to kill her, and of him she would make an example the story of which would spread through the tribes and send a shaft of terror into the heart of *all* shamans. The more they feared her, the more she could lead them into rash moves and flawed thinking.

All this must be done one step at a time though, if she could do it at all. It was not lost on her that she was merely a young girl, and her chances of success were lower than a hunter sneaking up on a pack of fen wolves in the open. Yet at the same time, she was also a symbol. She was the center point of all the forces among the Cheng that opposed the shamans. That must count for something. At least, she hoped so.

5. All Ways are Dangerous

The travelers were weary, but they were wary also. They moved slowly now, fearing an ambush set for them as much as the enemy coming up from behind.

Nerchak seemed to thrive in the situation. He found trails that few would, and ones that were difficult or impossible for riders to follow. Shar did not think they yet had reason to fear foot patrols. They were ahead of the enemy, and only riders could overtake them.

Dusk settled over the land, and Nerchak spoke to them during a brief rest.

"I know one more place where there are caves. If we can reach them, we should be safe there for the night. They're very hard to see if you don't know they're there."

"We'll get there," Kubodin answered, and he rested a hand on the blades of his axe.

They now went downhill into a gorge. As seemed to be common in this land, there were many dried up riverbeds. This one was a tumble of boulders, rockpools and trees stunted not by a lack of water but by growing in the cracks between rocks.

The path was concealed though, and impossible for a rider to traverse. It was dark here, even if night had not fallen elsewhere.

Yet Nerchak led them with confidence, and soon he took a turn to walk up a steep slope. At times, it was so steep that they had to climb with their arms, and Shar was glad when they came to a narrow path of stone. Climbing in the dark was dangerous.

The path did not last long. Soon they saw a cave entrance. It was large enough to pass through walking upright, but it was narrow. No one would see it from below at night, and probably not even in daylight.

It was a large cave inside, with a segment that ran deep toward the back. Firewood was stacked there, and there was a firepit too, the stones ringing its outside scorched and blackened. Yet it seemed to Shar that no fire had burned there for many years.

They risked lighting one. Little smoke would escape the cave, or much light. Against the chances of both, they used rocks to pin a cloak against the entrance as a kind of door.

When the fire was burning properly they noticed paintings on the wall. How these were made, Shar was not sure. Kubodin said they did something like this in the Wahlum Hills, using ocher.

The paintings were quite remarkable. There were scenes of hunting more than anything, both the hunter and the beasts being stalked. Yet there were images of farming too, and men with sickle blades to harvest wheat or barley. Livestock was shown as well, and there was a fierce looking breed of cattle that seemed massive and with long upturned horns. But that was not all.

There were scenes of war. Armies faced off against each other, and there were depictions of battlefields where the dead and wounded were piled up and vultures circled above. It seemed that no part of the Cheng empire, now or deep back into the past, had been without war. It saddened Shar, and she preferred to look at the other scenes and marveled at the skill of the painters who could create art in such primitive conditions.

But Asana, tranquil as he always was never missed anything when it came to weapons or armor.

"See," he pointed at one of the larger images of a battle, "even as it was on the stele we saw so it is here. These are not in the style of weapons that the Cheng have ever used. At least, that I know of."

Shar believed him. He knew these things, but it did make her wonder when these battles were fought and what people lived here before the Cheng. Suddenly, she had a revelation that the history she knew of her people and these lands was like looking at a single leaf and not realizing that it was merely part of a single tree within a forest of others.

They ate a quick meal by the swiftly dying fire. "How far is it to the Wahlum hills from here?" she asked. "If I learned my lessons well, it must be about four hundred miles."

Kubodin, as he so often did when they were at leisure, had his axe out and he was sharpening the blades. It did not seem to matter to him that they did not need it.

"Shulu taught you well. I'd say four hundred miles, perhaps a fly's jump more."

"It's a long way, and dangerous," she replied, thinking of all those miles and the chance of being spotted by an enemy for every one of them.

Kubodin shrugged. "All ways are dangerous."

"Maybe so, but perhaps we can cut down on the time that journey would take and give ourselves a better chance of eluding any pursuit into the bargain."

Kubodin paused what he was doing. "What do you suggest?"

"There are fishing villages not far from here, I think. If we head to the coast we might be able to hire a boat or ship and sail to the Wahlum Hills."

Asana leaned forward, rubbing his hands before the fire.

"I like that idea. A boat is swift and leaves no trail."

"Except for those at the shore who know, or can describe, who boarded her and where it sailed to," Nerchak put in. "But I can confirm there are fishing villages not that far away."

"I don't know about this coastline," Kubodin said, "but there's a fishing village on the north coast of the Wahlum Hills. It serves as a trading port, and it's quite large. It's not Two Ravens territory though, but from there we could get where we need to go quickly."

Shar thought about the information that had come out. It seemed to her that not only would sailing by ship cut their journey time, but it was the least likely way for them to be found. It was certainly true that booking a ship might see her recognized and leave a trail just as distinct in its way as walking over sand, but she could take precautions about that.

"Let's vote then," she said. "Who is for staying on land and traveling as we are?"

Nerchak raised his hand, and he looked about him as he did so but no one else agreed.

"Who is for taking a ship?" Shar continued.

She put up her own hand, and Asana and Kubodin did likewise.

"It's decided then." She glanced at Nerchak. "Will you lead us to the fishing village? I know you don't like the idea, but will you do it anyway?"

Those always-serious eyes of his held her own gaze, but then he smiled.

"Of course! You don't even have to ask. By sea or by land, I'm going with you no matter what."

It was good to know. She had not known him long, but he had impressed her and the way he had led them through this country was outstanding. If not for him, they might already have been discovered.

Going to the fishing village did present a major problem though. A warrior with two swords was not uncommon, but her violet eyes would give her away. She must find a way to hide them, if she could. But that would not be easy.

6. The Seer

The next morning dawned hot and clear.

Of the enemy, there was no sign. The travelers left the cave and scrambled down into the gorge. They replenished their water supplies, followed the ravine for some while until it became less steep on the sides, and then climbed out.

They headed north now, seeking the coastline. It was not that far away, but it was a rugged country and travel was slow. Continuing to try to hide their trail, and leave false trails where they could, slowed them even more.

This care was worth it though. They saw no more riders, nor patrols on foot for that matter. It was not by luck, but by the precautions they had already taken and Nerchak's skill.

Whatever doubts Shar had harbored about the young man were gone. Not only had he saved them, but he still guided them willingly and with good cheer despite their decision to seek a ship rather than heed his advice to continue traveling by land.

The day passed without event, yet in the afternoon clouds built up in the east, piling one upon another in a towering mass that rolled forward ominously.

"It's going to be a bad storm," Kubodin predicted. "We should seek shelter."

Shar looked into the mass of clouds, and saw the bottom of some tinged with a strange greenish blue color. Not only would there be a storm, it would likely come with hail also.

"Are there any more caves?" she asked Nerchak.

He shook his head. "Not here, but I'll find the best shelter I can. We might just be able to reach a good place."

They hastened ahead, and the towering bank of clouds grew higher and higher. It grew dark for the time of day, and gusts of wind picked up, swirling dust and leaves and then stilling momentarily only to start up again.

A roll of thunder boomed in the distance, and faded away to silence. There was nothing more for some time, and then lighting tore the sky and thunder trembled through the land a few long moments later.

They hurried forward, heads bent low into the wind when it came, and Shar scented the smell of rain. Lightning tore the sky again, closer this time, and the thunder boomed close on its heels.

"Hurry!" Asana called out.

"We're nearly there," Nerchak replied.

They climbed a steep slope, and Shar saw a curtain of rain in the distance. The trees began to bend too, and the wind that was gusty before now drove much harder and unceasingly.

Lightning flashed nearby and the crash of thunder seemed to heave the earth. They reached the top of the slope and entered a patch of trees. Rain was falling now, and it was bitterly cold. It grew heavier swiftly, and then a smattering of hail began.

The hail was small at first. It stopped momentarily, but a few moments later it came back, but it was bigger this time. Shar began to fear they would be seriously injured.

"Here!" Nerchak called, and even though he had shouted his voice was torn away by the wind and drowned by the roar of the trees and the smashing of hail against wood.

But as ever, Nerchak had led them well. There was a log cabin ahead, and though it looked an ancient and dilapidated thing, it was exactly what they needed.

Nerchak fumbled at the door, and then it opened. The rain pelted them all, and the hail grew larger. Just in time they all hastened in, and Nerchak closed the door behind them securing it with a bolt.

Outside, the wind howled and the lashing of trees was a constant roar only superseded by the smashing of hail against the roof. But it was dry here, and protected.

The travelers looked around and began to clean things up. It was a single room cabin, and there were no windows. It was a mess inside, with deep layers of dust and broken furniture, but there were a few chairs that were useable, and a hearth against the back wall.

They discarded their wet outer clothes and began to clean things up as best they could. All the while the storm raged outside, and Shar nearly felt sorry for those who pursued her. They were out there somewhere, and at least some of them would be feeling the full brunt of the storm. Her pity for them diminished quickly though. They would kill her on sight, if they could.

The storm seemed to subside outside, and they opened the door to have a quick look. The wind had died down, and the hail had ceased, but the rain still came down in torrents.

Water ran everywhere. The ground was awash, and several trees had fallen, the wind driving them down and the sodden soil around their roots giving way easily. Yet even as they looked, the wind picked up again and it seemed the storm began once more with a new fury.

"Nasty out there," Kubodin observed.

It was, but Shar was pleased. "All the better for us. Let the enemy suffer, and let whatever trail we left wash away. They'll not find it after this."

Asana moved over to have a look at the hearth, especially the chimney.

"It doesn't look blocked," he said, "and there's wood here. Let's start a fire."

It was a good idea, for they were cold and wet and there would be no enemy out in this. They would have gone to ground in the best place they could find, but it would not be good shelter like the cabin.

Asana got a blaze going, and though it was cramped in the small area they were soon feeling quite cheery while the storm raged outside.

They sat around the fire after dinner and talked quietly. The storm was passing, but the rain continued unabated.

"We're getting close to the coast now," Nerchak told them. "This is no doubt a hunter's cabin, and there will be farms and villages soon, if isolated ones."

"And shamans?" Shar asked.

"Shamans are everywhere."

That was true, and Shar did not like it. It would be one thing to be recognized because of her eyes by a farmer, but another thing by a shaman. The farmer might well love her, but the shaman would try to kill her. Or worse, send word for help.

She touched the hilts of her swords. They were not just weapons of steel, but would offer protection against magic too. Even so, her best chance of survival was to remain hidden as long as possible while she gathered an army.

The night wore on, and the storm faded away to rumblings in the distance. The rain weakened too, but it did not stop.

They laid out their cloaks on the floor, fed the fire once more, and then slept. Shar lay awake for a little while, loving the sound of the rain on the roof and feeling for the first time in a long while that she was in a place like home. The hot day and the storm, followed by a cold night, was just as it was back in Tsarin Fen, and she felt a longing to return there and to see Shulu.

But Shulu was gone from the fen, likely hunted as she was herself, and her home was now wherever she lay down to sleep at night, which would never be the same place twice in a row.

Shar drifted away to oblivion, and knew nothing more until dawn broke the next day.

It was a bright dawn. The rain had ceased, if only a few hours earlier, and the sky was mostly clear with a few scattered clouds still left.

The ground was sodden, and travel would be difficult. Yet they thought it better to strike out now for the coast as quickly as possible.

"We'll leave a trail that cannot be hidden," Nerchak warned.

"True," Shar agreed. "But the enemy would have to be close to find and follow it. If they find it at all. With luck, it might take them days, or even longer, to search this area. And when they do, the trail might just as easily be hunters as us."

They pressed ahead. The day warmed up quickly, and it grew humid as well. It really did remind Shar of the fen, at least the way it felt. The landscape was quite different though.

The slope of the ground was mostly downhill toward the coast, and the cover of trees grew quickly thinner. By noon, they had reached an area where there were scattered farms, and here and there were plumes of smoke that came from isolated homesteads or small villages.

There were roads too. At first, they were little more than muddy trails but they soon widened. These, the travelers avoided. Likewise any contact with farmers.

At one point they came near to a group of woodcutters, but the noise of their activity rang through the air and they were easily avoided.

"One more day and we'll be at the fishing village," Nerchak told them.

The sooner the better, as far as Shar was concerned. She wanted to board a boat and disappear on the waves where they could not be tracked. She would just have to find a way to disguise her violet eyes.

The ground remained muddy, especially as they avoided the roads that were firmer and better drained. The others did not like it and complained, but Shar merely laughed. It was normal for her having grown up in the fen, and it was a discomfort she was so used to that she did not even notice it.

The land grew flatter as they went, and everywhere they began to see signs of people. There were roads, and often they could see several plumes of smoke not too far away. There was livestock too, often being herds of goats but sometimes cattle. They stayed clear of these where they could. No doubt there would be people tending them.

"Take cover!" Asana warned unexpectedly as they descended a grassy slope into a wood. Everyone reacted quickly, following his lead and running the last little bit until they were under the protection of the trees.

"What is it?" Nerchak asked. He had drawn his sword and he looked like he knew how to use it.

Shar had already guessed before Asana answered.

"An eagle," the swordmaster replied.

It was impossible to know if they were being overly cautious, but Shar thought it for the best to stay under cover. They had experienced great luck with the storm that would hide their trail, and the last thing they needed now was to be spied through the air. That would unravel their luck completely, and it was better to risk a delay than exposure to their enemy.

They found a patch of thickly growing trees, and there they waited. All except Asana, who crawled a little way away until he found an open patch where there were only ferns, but they still offered him a place to conceal himself. There he lay down on his back and watched the sky between the green fronds.

"What's it doing?" Kubodin asked.

"What eagles do," Asana replied. "Circling the high skies slowly. What did you expect?"

"Very funny."

Shar suppressed a smile. She had watched these two since she had first met them. For all that they were completely opposite in every possible way, and despite their banter, she did not think she had ever met two greater friends. Each, she thought, would die for the other.

The minutes wore on, and Shar shrugged away the impatience she felt. The eagle would not stay there forever, and when it was out of sight they could go on again. Until then, she might as well enjoy a rest.

Shar lay back and began to doze. A fly bothered her, trying to land again and again on her face. In the distance she heard the bellowing of cattle, but it was faint and far away. It was peaceful here, and she liked it. The many lands of the Cheng were all different, but each was good in its own way.

Asana sat up amidst the ferns a little while later. "It's gone," he advised.

They came to their feet then, still warily looking at the sky, and moved on.

The country soon became almost flat, and the woods were far fewer. If another eagle came into sight, they would not have much in the way of cover. And heading for it might only reveal that they wanted to hide and draw suspicion onto them. Assuming the eagle was more than an eagle, anyway.

It was not long before they came to a road. This was wider than the others, and likely served as the main route into the village. They avoided it.

It was well that they did. Walking parallel to it, but half a mile away, they could still see any other travelers. There were a few of those. There was a farmer with a cart and a little while later a group of children. Then from the direction of the village they saw a large group of riders. There was a half dozen of them, and Nerchak came to a stop behind a bush.

They lay down, for the bush gave little cover, and just lifting their heads sightly they watched the riders move up the road in their direction.

"Nazram," Kubodin said.

Nerchak cast a sideways glance at him. "How can you tell from this distance?"

"I can smell them."

Nerchak raised his eyebrows at that, but gave no answer. As the riders drew level though, the little hill man was proved correct. There was no uniform for nazram, but they always had the best clothes and equipment. Without doubt, most of them also carried themselves with a certain arrogance.

Shar glanced at Kubodin. It was clear that he hated the nazram, and no doubt there was a history there. If nothing else, the way he fingered his axe just now gave it away. He almost looked like he was about to charge to the road and attack them single handedly.

No one moved, however, and the riders passed on and went out of sight. What they were doing was not obvious though.

"A patrol?" suggested Shar.

"Maybe," Asana replied. He did not seem convinced though. Nor was Shar. The nazram were the personal soldiers of the shaman they were assigned to, and they did not leave their master's side often. Most likely, these men were on more than a patrol – they were looking for her. That did not mean they knew she was here though. They might just have been sent out to scout on the possibility she had come this way. After all, if things were well, then the shamans did not know where they were at all, and therefore must search everywhere.

The travelers moved on after that, but they went warily. There were fewer and fewer places to hide, and more and more often there were people moving about. It was increasingly difficult to avoid them without drawing suspicion.

This slowed them down greatly. Even more so when they had to go out of their way to avoid a village, and in the process of doing that they had to avoid a neighboring village that was unusually close.

They spent the night in a small wood on a hill. From it they could see if anyone approached yet remain hidden themselves. They did not dare light a fire though.

"We're close to the fishing village by the coast," Nerchak said. "If we leave at first light, we'll reach it within an hour, maybe a touch more."

"Then it's time I disguised myself," Shar said. "From tomorrow onward we can no longer avoid people."

Asana nodded. "I've been thinking you'll need to do something. Those eyes of yours … they're startling. How will you do it?"

Shar had given it much thought, and there were several options. The best, she had decided, was the one least expected. For surely the shamans must anticipate that she would try to hide.

She drew out of an inner pocket a long strip of white cloth that she had prepared.

"Meet Namaya, the seer."

As she spoke she wrapped the cloth in a band around her eyes and tied it at the back of her head. This, she hoped, would be enough. It not only hid her eyes but changed the look of her face too.

7. Remember Me

The cloth around her eyes was thick enough to obscure most of Shar's vision, but she could still see the broad outline of things. It would disguise her, and hinder her enough that she would actually seem blind, but allow her some ability to perceive what was happening around her.

"Well, what do you think?"

"It'll work," Asana replied.

"I think so too," Kubodin agreed.

She turned to Nerchak. "What do you think?"

The young man looked thoughtful. "It should work for your eyes, but what about your swords? Seers don't wear swords – especially two of them. Nor with amethyst like that set in their pommels."

Shar took the cloth away from her eyes. "Good points, both," she replied. "But there's a temple in the Skultic Mountains, far to the west, where the monks are trained as warriors, and where some specialize in the arts of the seer."

"I didn't know that," he said.

She flashed him a smile. "Nor will those we meet, but they'll believe when I tell them just as you did."

Kubodin laughed, but Nerchak did not look so happy that he had been fooled.

"Don't feel too bad," she said. "There really was such a temple there once. Everything I said was true, but so far as I know the monastery died out a few hundred years ago."

"What about the pommels though?"

Shar knew he was right. They would give her away as much as her own eyes would. But her grandmother had told her much about the magic in the swords, and there was something she had been thinking of trying. She had put it off because, though the magic in the swords would be of great help to her, it came from a demon trapped in the metal and she wanted nothing to do with that. It was bad enough that it was there, but to communicate with it was worse.

She slid her hands down to the hilts and covered the bright amethyst with her palms. *Hide the jewels*, she commanded silently.

There was a sensation of heat against her skin, and she felt the magic of the blades stir. Then it was gone, and she withdrew her hands.

"Fascinating," Nerchak said.

Shar looked down. The violet stones were gone now, and the pommel looked nothing more than a dark sphere of metal.

They spent an uneventful night then, each taking turns to keep watch. They were too close now to an area densely populated not to do so.

By first light the next day they were already traveling, and soon they could avoid neither roads nor people at all. So they did not try to. Instead, they walked boldly down the largest road, and greeted people in friendly fashion.

Shar wore the strip of cloth about her eyes, and Nerchak acted as a kind of guide. Just like the seer she had met in the mountains, Shar affected that despite her physical blindness she could see by the use of magic.

People bowed to her on the road, for seers were rare and much respected. Yet some of these people made various signs intended to avert evil when they thought they were out of sight.

Shar did not mind. Seers *were* respected, but it was said that their tidings of the future were often dark and not accepted well by those who asked for it to be read.

They walked through well cultivated farmlands now, and trod wearily up a slope. When they came to its crest they stopped. Before them lay a very large village, and beyond it the sea.

There was no one close, and Shar lifted up her blindfold. Shulu had described the sea to her, and she had learned of ships and boats. She understood their uses, both for trade and war. She understood the sea was a vast resource of many kinds of food that were unavailable inland. Nothing prepared her for the way the sea looked though.

It was a still morning, and the sky was clear. Light sparkled on countless little wave crests, and the breath of the ocean was salty against her face. There was something beautiful about it, yet at the same time something that spoke of sorrow and eternity. It was like an old woman who had seen all that life had to offer a thousand times over. It was beyond Shar's comprehension. It had been before her, and would be after her. It recked nothing of people, nor emperor's nor the petty squabbles of humanity.

"It's beautiful," she said.

Kubodin raised his eyebrows. "I guess so. At least if you go in for that sort of thing. I'd rather the hills though. Or a woman with a smile on her face and the word yes on her lips. That's beauty!"

Asana sighed. "Pay no heed to him. He has the soul of a warrior and not a poet."

Kubodin shrugged. "Poetry hasn't ever defended me from an enemy."

Shar ignored them and kept looking at the vastness of what lay before her, and wondered what other shores there were beyond her sight.

"Someone is coming up behind us," Nerchak warned.

Reluctantly, Shar put her blindfold back in place and they began their descent into the village.

It did not take long. Every step they took the smell of the village became stronger. At first, this was only the fresh scent of the sea. Soon though there were less pleasant odors. Chief among them the stench of rotting fish.

They wandered through the streets, not long ago muddy but now churned by the passage of many feet and carts. Chickens darted everywhere, and there was a strange bird that Shar had never seen before. It was supremely agile in the gusty breeze from the sea as well as loud and raucous.

Nerchak saw her studying them through her blindfold as best she could.

"They're seagulls," he told her.

They navigated the village without incident. Most people did not give them more than a passing look, though a few studied Shar with curiosity. There did not seem to be any recognition though.

After a while the road zigzagged down to the shore, and the crashing of the waves grew loud. Here, there was a long pier, and beside it were tied a large number of boats. Farther along there was a second pier.

They walked along the pier and passed several smaller boats. When they came to a larger one Asana called out to the deck hands who were busy there.

"Taking any passengers?"

"No," came the reply. "We fish only."

They did not seem too friendly, but Shar reasoned they were just busy. Strangers in Tsarin Fen were always treated with respect though. Then again, strangers were likely a lot more common here than there.

Asana asked the same question several more times with the same result. They found a friendly crew member on one of the last boats on the pier however, and he talked to them for a while about the weather and the prospects of trade, but they were headed west instead of east. He did offer them some information though.

"Look for Captain Tsergar on the next pier. His is the biggest boat there, and I believe he's headed eastward on the afternoon tide."

They thanked him and retraced their steps. It took a while, for the pier was long. It was also old and falling apart. The next pier seemed nearly new, and though it did not have as many boats tethered to it, they were larger.

The largest one was quite clear to see though. It was also the last one at the far end. They came to it, and saw a large crew busy loading on chests. What was in them, Shar did not know. But they seemed heavy, for two men carried each and they seemed to struggle.

"Ahoy the ship!" Asana called.

A deckhand looked across at them and stopped tying the rope he was working on.

"What can I do for you?"

"We're looking for passage eastward. Is captain Tsergar available?"

The deckhand studied them a moment, his eyes lingering on Shar.

"He's below deck. I'll fetch him."

The sailor moved away and was gone a little while. He did not come back, but a young man did. He was short and squat of build, but a curved sword hung at his side such as seamen often used, and it looked of fine quality with a ruby set in the pommel.

The man leaned against a rope, holding it with one hand and looking at them lazily. It was a posture that might indeed be taken for laziness, but Shar knew better. He had the look of a warrior: relaxed and at ease but ready to leap into action swifter than thought at need. There was a shrewd glint in his gaze too.

"I'm Captain Tsergar."

"We're looking for passage," Asana told him. "Eastward to the Wahlum Hills. Are you going there?"

The captain studied them all slowly before he answered.

"That I am. At least, that's where I'm headed first. And I have room, maybe, for passengers if you don't mind a bit of a squeeze. But travelers are rare these days. I can't guarantee your safety. The sea can be dangerous, but you'll find the hills much more so."

Asana gave one of his nonchalant shrugs that was so small that sometimes people did not even notice it.

"What place *is* safe these days? We have business there though, and we'll chance it if you'll take us."

The captain looked them over again, and Shar did not doubt that he was a fine judge of character. He would also know that more was going on here than it seemed, but he had no inclination to find out. Knowledge was power, but it was also dangerous and sometimes ignorance was better. He would send them away if he thought they would bring him trouble, but likewise few people in business passed by the opportunity to earn more coin.

For a while he and Asana bargained over the fare to be charged, but came to an acceptable agreement readily enough.

"We're done then," the captain said. "Except for one thing only. Let the seer tell my fortune, and if I like it we have a deal."

Asana hesitated, but Shar lifted her head and gazed straight at the captain. She knew that such a thing could be unsettling, and she wanted to put him on the back foot. Without doubt, this was a test. He did not wish to have his future told. This was to see if she really was the seer she appeared to be, and in no way could she fail to prove that to him or they would get no passage and it would arouse his suspicions. Word of such a thing would come swiftly to the ears of the local shaman too.

She slowly raised her hand and pointed at him. She did not see the gazes of the others, but she felt the pressure of them against her. They held their breath waiting on her performance.

"My name is Namaya, and though blind the gods gift me with sight. You cannot hide from me. Your thoughts are open to my mind, and your future is laid out to me even as you use the stars to navigate your ship. Do you seek to know your fate? Do you dare to lift up the veil of the gods and see the face of destiny?"

Shulu had taught her the way of seers, and she had trained her in the arts of oratory. At the words she had spoken she sensed a change in the captain. He did not believe in such things, yet still she had spoken in a way to nurture the seed of doubt in his mind.

After a pause, he answered. He did not shift posture, but she felt a change in his attitude.

"I seek to know my future. Tell me, O seer with the sight of the gods, what awaits this humble trader on the seas?"

Shar raised both her hands, and she lifted up her head as though inviting communion with the powers of the heavens.

"A trader you are, but the gods see more. Nor are you humble. A great spirit burns within you, and you know it. Now, you trade the seas, but I see a day when your cargo will not be goods but soldiers. No passengers will you bear, save Death himself. The sea will run red beneath your sails, and your ship will strive in battle with ships of the enemy. The world changes, and you must pick a side. Choose wisely, and glory and wealth will come to you. Choose poorly, and you shall rest in a seafarer's grave beneath the waves."

A hush fell over the ship, and the crew looked at their captain with a certain awe. For the captain's part, he gazed back at her and pretended indifference, but she saw the quicker rise and fall of his chest that revealed excitement.

"Is there anything else?" he asked.

Shar drew herself up and trembled, but her voice rang clear above the tumult of the sea and the piercing cries of the strange white birds that rode the wind currents above it.

"I see you choosing the right side, that which is favored by destiny in the battles to be. Verily, you will do a single deed that enshrines you as a hero and that will earn you glory and fame. Your name will endure a thousand years. When you have done it, think back to this moment and remember it. For it was I, Namaya the Seer, who foretold it."

Shar finished speaking and allowed herself to droop as though spent. She hoped she had done enough to convince him. Most men were easily fooled. Tell them a tale of their own glory and they were apt to believe it. Even so, he seemed the sort of man who might just do the things she had foretold.

"Come aboard," the captain invited. "The ship will sail within a few hours."

The travelers did so, Nerchak guiding Shar carefully over the narrow plank between pier and ship. She felt relief. At last they would be away from the searchers seeking them, and she did not think that any would realize that Namaya the Seer and Shar of the Fen Wolf tribe, descendant of Chen Fei, were one and the same.

She could see dimly despite the strip of cloth over her eyes, and the gazes of the crew were filled with a primitive fear of her. Some of them would summon the courage to hear her pronouncements of their fate during the voyage, but not many.

8. The Woman in Black

The captain was true to his word, and within hours the ship slowly moved out to sea, the cloth of its sails taut and its prow riding proud over the waters.

The travelers had spent that time in a cramped cabin below deck, but the time passed swiftly in quiet conversation.

"How did you do that foretelling?" Asana asked. "I have met several seers before, and you captured the mood they present to an audience perfectly."

Shar sent out a silent prayer of thanks to her grandmother.

"Shulu trained me in many things. The ways of seers was one of them. Perhaps not so much to give a performance like that, but to understand how a seer, or one who pretended to be so, might manipulate me. But to best understand the tricks one has to perform them. They are useful not just for that but oratory in general."

Asana seemed impressed, and Kubodin looked at her quizzically.

"Are you sure it was performance only? You had me fooled."

"None of my predictions have ever come true before. I don't think this will either." She did wonder as she answered though. Something had felt strange about it, and just maybe some talent had woken in her. Or been woken by the presence of the magic in the swords. Then she dismissed such thoughts, for she knew exactly why she had said what she had said and how she had chosen the wording she thought would best impress the captain.

What man did not like to hear predictions about his future glory? She felt guilty over that, but there was no other way if she wished to remain hidden.

The ship did not go far out to sea. Few Cheng vessels ever did. For the most part, they hugged the coastline and traded from village to village or fished the abundant waters.

It was drawing on to dusk when the ship turned eastward, and that change of direction did not feel good to Shar. They went out onto the deck, and nausea hit her fast, but she breathed deep and held it in check as best she could. Asana and Kubodin moved closer to the rails in case they were going to be sick, but Nerchak merely laughed at them. He seemed his normal self, and Shar wondered if he was just naturally unaffected by the heaving of the boat or if he had experience of sea travel before.

They stayed clear of the sailors and let them do their tasks in peace, but every once in a while one of the men grinned at them, knowing how they felt and seemingly amused by it.

The stars kindled in the sky, the friends of mariners and travelers alike, and the sigh of the sea was everywhere. It was a new world to Shar, and she envied the captain and his men. Here was freedom and the joy of travel, and no man was lord of others. Even the captain, she had learned, was not so because money or position had put him there. The crew owned the ship together, he among them, and they elected a leader to be their captain. If his leadership did not please them, he would resume duties as a crew member and another would be chosen to take his place.

Even as she thought of him, the captain approached her. She still wore her cloth disguise, and it was dark, but she knew him by his firm step. Also, she had been expecting him. Those for whom the future had been foretold felt afterward the need to confirm if it was true. So at least Shulu had told her.

"Greetings, Captain."

If he had been surprised at her recognition of him, he did not mention it. Nor was Shar worried that it would give her away. Rather it would increase the aura of otherworldliness about her.

"Is the cabin to your liking, Seeress Namaya?"

"It will serve me well. My needs are simple. Tell me, how long will it take to reach the coast of the Wahlum Hills?"

The captain did not sit down next to her. That would be unseemly, and whatever else he was, whether that was sailor, smuggler or pirate, for usually to be one was to be all the others at need, he understood the etiquette allowed to seers or those who possessed magic. Instantly, that made her wary.

"It depends on the weather, but I should think three days with luck. Probably four, for luck is never consistent on the seas."

She could no longer see them, but she could hear Asana and Kubodin chatting a little way off. Their conversation was quiet and carefree, but she knew their attention was all on the captain and her. The disguise she used might not fool anyone warned to keep watch for a girl with two swords.

"Do you like the sea?" the captain asked.

"I love it. I have come to love all the lands I travel, even if in this case the *land* is over water."

He laughed at that, and she liked the sound of it. She liked *him*, but she did not trust him. Trust, Shulu had warned her, was a snare for the unwary. It must be earned, and once broken could never be mended.

"I love it too," he answered. "I wasn't born a sailor though. My father was a fisherman, but it was the nazram

I joined when old enough. I was good with a sword, you see."

Shar felt that sense of wariness turn to alarm. He had not come to her to discuss the foretelling.

She gave no answer, but merely waited. He studied her for a moment, and then leaned forward and whispered so softly that even she could barely hear it. No one else would.

"I still have friends in the nazram, if few. I know who you are."

It was all Shar could do to remain still, but she did so and waited. If this man truly knew who she was, why had he not alerted the village shaman when they were at the pier?

The captain went on. "Your name is Shar, and you are a descendant of the emperor. You are no seer, but rather a warrior. I know one when I see one, and the two swords you carry are the twin swords of your ancestor."

Shar tilted her head as though she were amused. "What a novel idea! But not one, I fear, the shamans would like."

She saw the flash of his smile in the dark, for she had worked the cloth strip up slightly in case she needed to fight.

"Perhaps it *is* a novel idea at that. Yet if I'm wrong, you can prove it easily. Show me your eyes. If you're blind, I will apologize."

He had her there, and she knew it. She could protest, but they both knew that would be a sham. To refuse was to accept his accusation. To accede was to prove it too, for though it was dark there was still enough light, from both the stars and the lantern on to the prow, for him to tell their color.

"And do the crew believe as you do?" she asked.

"They believe you to be a seer, and nothing more. I haven't told them what I know."

Shar hesitated, but she could not refuse. This man *knew*, and it was better that she tried to control the situation rather than to let it run its course.

"Then look into my eyes, if you dare. Once you do so, your life will never be the same again."

She drew away the cloth and gazed at him with the violet eyes that had long been death to any who possessed them. It was said that her ancestor used his gaze to influence people, for there was a mystique to such an unusual color, and some believed there was magic in them.

"Look into my eyes," she commanded. "I am your emperor-to-be, and I have need of you. Will you aid me?"

The captain became still as stone. Farther away, Asana and Kubodin had stopped talking, and she knew they were ready to fight and unleash death upon the ship. But she looked only on the captain, her eyes boring into his own as though there truly were magic in them and she was invoking it.

Tsergar sighed. "I have seen enough. Place the cloth back, my lady."

Shar did so, without haste. She said nothing.

The silence grew between them, but at length the captain broke it.

"I will serve you, emperor-to-be. I fear it will lead to my death, but there are many such as I who are dissatisfied with the ways of the shamans and of the nazram that lick their boots but lord it over others. We would see a change."

"Change is coming," Shar answered. "The age of the shamans draws to a close."

He studied her. "Can you beat them?"

"It is my destiny to do so. I will need your help though. For now, that means silence. But later, when you hear I have raised an army, come to me. I will need such as you."

They spoke no more, and a moment later the captain left her. She had felt great fear at first, but then a sense of rightness had settled over her. She *would* need this man somehow in the future. He would *not* betray her.

She and the others went below deck after that, and she whispered to them what had happened. They were worried, but her heart was light. Of Tsergar she was certain, and she trusted him.

The days passed and Shar never quite shook off the nausea that beset her on the ship. She ate little. She appeared seldom on deck, but wherever she went at least one of the others went with her. But no one approached her, not even the captain, and all seemed well.

On the fourth morning the ship tacked closer to land, and Shar studied the country they headed for. She could see little. All seemed wreathed in mist, but she caught glimpses here and there of densely forested hills.

Kubodin was near her on the deck, and the little hill man's hand caressed his axe. He gazed keenly at what lay ahead, and his eyes were fierce as an eagle's.

"You're coming home, Kubodin."

He did not take his gaze off the land. "I am, and some will welcome me, but not all. There will be great trouble."

The ship drew up to a pier, and beyond it, unveiled of the mists that swirled higher up in the hills, a village sprawled. It was just such a fishing village as they had come from, only smaller. Yet it was farther away from the searching shamans, and here Shar hoped she would be unknown for some time. And when her enemies did learn of her, it would take them time to travel here.

The crew laid out a plank to the pier, and men waited there to receive the ship's cargo. First though, the captain called for the travelers and escorted them from the ship. They said such farewells as would be expected of passengers and captain, but Tsergar's eyes held a knowing look, and a thoughtful one. Shar brushed his shoulder as she passed by, an unspoken sign of what had passed between them, and she felt him tense at the touch.

Then they were away and briskly walking along the pier toward the village.

The pier was crowded. Many had come to help unload cargo, and another vessel must have arrived only a little earlier. It was a fishing vessel, and a large one.

They exited the pier and came into the village. It was crowded and busy, and Shar did not much care for it. Nerchak led her by the hand, but they came to a pause.

"Where to?" the young man asked.

Kubodin grunted. "I've not been here either. The sooner we get through the village and out into the wilder lands beyond the safer it'll be for us. We seem to be on a main road, so I suggest we follow it. It should be the quickest way through to the other side."

They adopted this advice and moved on. The street was crowded, and as far as Shar could see the people looked much like Cheng everywhere across the land. Yet they seemed shorter here, and squatter. They reminded her of Kubodin, and though this was not his tribe most likely they were closely related.

They walked through the center of the village without incident, but soon after Nerchak came to a halt. The crowd had thinned now, but ahead of them a group of men had gathered, and though Shar could not see them properly she had her suspicions.

Kubodin confirmed them. "Nazram," he muttered darky, and there was anger in his voice.

A moment everything seemed to stand still, then the nazram charged at them and from out of an alleyway behind them another group emerged, swords drawn.

"They're nazram from my tribe," Kubodin cried out, and his great axe was in his hand and the light of battle in his eyes.

Shar drew one of her swords, but not both. She did not wish to reveal herself if she could help it. If these men were here to kill, it might be to strike against Kubodin. They may not even know who she was.

But she lifted the cloth about her eyes a little, and then the crash of steel rang in the air. All about them the villagers fled, and doors slammed shut quickly. Battle cries thundered and curses and screams followed.

For a moment, all was chaos. The great axe of Kubodin flashed through the air, and death followed it. Heads rolled to the muddy ground, and blood spurted.

Nerchak moved with blinding speed, and two dead men lay before him. Asana was faster still, and Shar, despite her disadvantage, killed a man too. Her sword severed a limb and cut deep into the neck of her opponent.

The nazram hesitated, clearly taken by surprise, and fell back a little. Kubodin shouted and leaped among them, but they withdrew even more. In doing so, an opening into an alley to the left became apparent. But Shar was not sure if escape lay that way, or if it were a trap.

"Kubodin!" Asana yelled, for the little man fought in a great frenzy, and he was at risk of being cut off from his friends and surrounded by the enemy. Yet however fierce the fey spirit that drove him was, it was not without reason. He saw his danger, slew one more man with an unexpected upward thrust that disemboweled him, spilling blood and guts to the road, and then retreated back toward the others.

Shar was still in doubt, but even at that moment the voice of her grandmother seemed to rise up in their midst.

"The alley, fools. Go down the alley!"

Shar was startled beyond measure, yet straightaway she turned her feet toward that opening and hastened toward it. The others followed, and even as they did so a shadow figure stood within it, all rags and bone, and beckoned for them to follow.

The figure disappeared, and Shar raced after it as fast as she could run. The sound of their race thundered over the hard-packed surface of the road, and it echoed back to them from the walls of the close by huts and cottages.

Ahead, Shar saw the figure again. It was closer now, and it leaped and danced madly as it fled, the tattered clothes around it streaming behind. Yet it slowed, beckoned again, and turned down another alley.

They followed. Pursuit was coming up behind them, but the nazram had been surprised and were some way back. And they would have heard the voice as well, and perhaps seen the shadowy figure. Superstition might have slowed their steps also.

In this new alley a strange mist rose up from the earth, and even as they ran over it, it billowed higher and filled the shadowy way.

Yet again, the figure was before them, closer than ever. The tattered cloak was black, and the hood was pulled up. But a bony hand beckoned at them once more, and there was another turn down a different alley.

They hastened after it. Shar was almost as afraid of it as of those who came behind, for though it seemed like Shulu it could not be. No matter how fast they raced after it, always it was ahead. It flittered over the road like a thing of spirit rather than flesh, and despite the hidden physical strength of her grandmother, she could not outpace them like that.

They ran through a series of alleys, turning and twisting, and ever the mist came up after to hide them. The enemy had fallen back, bemused, and the travelers escaped them, at least for now. Yet Shar wondered who this person was who guided them, if it were even a live person at all.

9. Always Silent

Shar ran ahead, and the others were close to her. Here and there they startled people, but they did not slow down.

The mysterious mist was gone. So too were their pursuers. They had been lost somewhere back in the maze of alleyways and narrow roads. They would still be there, though.

They slowed to a fast walk so as to stop drawing attention.

"How could they have found us?" Nerchak asked.

Shar thought she knew the answer, and Kubodin confirmed it.

"They weren't after Shar," the little man said. "They were from my tribe. They were Two Ravens' nazram, and they were after me."

Nerchak seemed dissatisfied with that. "Maybe so, but why would they care about you? And even if they did, how could they know you were coming?"

Ahead of them the mysterious figure was still there guiding them on. But now it seemed more like just a shadow, and no one else seemed to see it but the travelers.

"The nazram … let's just say they don't like me," Kubodin replied. "How they knew I was returning here, I don't know. I suspect the clan's shaman Drasta Gan sent them though. And he's rumored to converse with the dead and to learn much of the future."

That worried Shar. Yet it had not seemed that the nazram had paid any special attention to her. It might be that this Drasta Gan did not know of her yet. She hoped so, but time would tell.

"They may not have been the only nazram," Asana said. "We must expect others, and that maybe all ways out of this village are guarded."

It was a sobering thought, but the more Shar considered it the more likely it seemed. If this Drasta knew by his arts that Kubodin was coming, he would cast a net around the village. It was a lot of resources to spend against one man, but if he hated him enough, or feared him enough, it might be so.

Shar indicated the figure ahead of them, seemingly nothing more than a tattered shadow now.

"Our savior, whoever or whatever it is, has led us well so far. Nor has it gone yet, but still wants us to follow. So I think we should trust our luck to that, and if all ways out of the village are guarded, then maybe it knows a way to slip past."

No one objected. That did not mean they thought it was a good idea. It only indicated they had no better plan.

The figure *did* keep leading them, and the route was roundabout. Yet it became clear soon enough that they had turned around and headed back down toward the sea. The smell of it was strong again, but they came down to it by different paths than they had come up from it.

About them the village seemed to change. It was less prosperous, though that would not be hard. The people were dirty and unoccupied, and the huts were in ill repair.

When they came to the beach though they were not near the pier. They had come some quarter of a mile east of it, and a rugged coastline was before them with the sound of the waves crashing loudly into a series of cliffs.

The dark figure was before them still, mysterious as always but now that they had left people behind it seemed more real again.

"I don't trust it," Nerchak said. "We should turn back."

Kubodin peered ahead at it. "I don't trust it either, but going back is no plan. Those streets and alleys will be full of nazram searching for us."

The figure led them along the beach, and Shar noticed it left no tracks. She did not say anything, but she was not alone in noticing. All the others had too, for they drew their weapons. Shar alone did not, yet she itched to do so.

They soon came to the cliffs, only the base of the nearest one was hollowed out by the pounding of the sea when the tide was higher. Just at the moment the entrance was free of water though.

The figure beckoned again, and then went inside. For several moments they all hesitated, and then Shar summoned her courage and walked forward. The others came behind her.

It was dark in the cave, but not completely. It was bigger than it looked, and the floor was wet with deep puddles in places. It was no place to be caught when the tide came in.

Of the figure, there was no sign.

They hesitated momentarily, but soon their eyes adjusted to the poor light and they could see more. The rear of the cave was a jagged series of hollows where erosion had done its work, but also vertical ridges of harder stone that were more resistant.

On one of the ridges the shadowy figure stood, and it beckoned again. Then it turned and seemed to dissolve into the stone, but Shar soon realized it was another cave.

They clambered up to follow, and it was awkward for the stone was wet and slippery. Again, there was no way her grandmother could have climbed this, and Shar knew she must have misheard that voice earlier. It could not be her.

They came to the ledge on which the figure had stood. It was small and narrow, and they could barely all fit on it at once. Together they looked into the new cave.

It was black as midnight, yet even as they looked that mist that they had seen earlier in the alleys rose again. It lifted from the floor of the tunnel like steam from a boiling pot, only this time there was a luminescence to it and they could see enough to continue.

No one said the obvious. Should they be led deep into the tunnel, where there would probably be branches and offshoots, and then the light taken away they might well die in there unable to find their way out.

Kubodin was the first to move. "We've come this far. We might as well go all the way."

Even as he spoke he moved ahead, but his axe was in his hand and held before him in a ready position.

They followed him, and this time Shar came up the rear. It was her normal position, and as always she looked and listened for any sign of the nazram.

There was nothing. Yet still, she had a feeling they would not so easily give up. All it would take would be a few questions here and there in the village, and they could trace their quarry to the beach. From there they could track them to this very spot. But what then?

Mysterious, or even sinister as the figure appeared, it had saved them up until now. And in these caves, where there was no light, it would save them again. By the time the nazram fetched torches from back in the village it would be too late to follow.

So Shar hoped. Yet she did not know what was ahead, and the figure *was* in some way sinister. It never showed its face, and it had not spoken except for that one time.

They moved onward, and their fears were quickly grounded in reality. Again and again there were offshoots to the tunnel. Many were small. Some so small that only a child could pass through them. Others were larger though, and they soon knew they were lost except for the figure, always silent, always beckoning them on, and the faint path of the mist leading forward.

They were deep in the earth now, and Shar did not like it. She could see the faces of the others faintly at times, and they did not seem disturbed. That was a mask though. She knew them well enough now to understand that they showed no fear, least of all when it was strong upon them.

It was the same with Nerchak as the others, but at him she marveled. He was younger than the rest of them, yet of them all he seemed the least worried. They could all be going for a stroll to stretch their legs after breakfast instead of risking their lives, but if so, he was the one who whistled blithely as he walked.

The series of caves seemed to have no end. Shar did not think they had been down here that long, but she found it hard to judge the passing of time with nothing to measure it by in the unending dark and weariness of clambering through twisting tunnels.

Yet the tunnels were not always the same. At one place it opened out into a vast cave, and the faint light did not show the walls to any side. Yet by the eerie echoing in the chamber Shar knew there were walls, and made some guess that they were a hundred feet away to either side.

She never saw them though. At her feet however she trod solid stone, rather than the rock-strewn and sandy paths of before. Nor was it an ordinary stone, but it ran with veins of minerals that gleamed and glinted in varied colors. There was no sign that anyone had ever been here though. There had been no signs of fires where someone had sought shelter, even back near the beach. There were no paintings on the wall. There was nothing.

How then, she wondered, did that black figure who led them know the way herself? Had she somehow trod and learned this strange path beneath the earth that others did not seem to dare? Or divined it by magic? Or was she a creature of the dark deeps of the earth herself, and not human at all?

10. Betrayal

The travelers did not stop, and they grew tired. Every step became difficult, for the way grew narrow and the ground which they trod was uneven.

Worse, the mist that gave light began to fade.

Yet they continued on. At times they could not see the figure that led them. It was faint as a shadow, and there were many of those.

They had long since sheathed their weapons. There was no foe down here to fight. The enemy was darkness. No steel could slay that, nor find a way out of the terrible maze.

"A rest wouldn't hurt us," Kubodin muttered. "But if we stop now, the figure we follow might soon disappear and leave us here."

Shar thought he was right. That figure, whatever it was, could be no person. She had guessed so all along. It was a thing of magic, even if she did not know whose. And the power that drove it seemed to be weakening. Soon, they would be alone.

The interminable journey continued, yet unexpectedly the radiance of the mist grew stronger again. Shar could not fathom it.

"Is it just me?" she asked. "Or is the figure giving us more light again?"

"No and no," Asana replied in his soft voice, but there was a hint of eagerness in it. "The figure is gone, I think. The magic that formed it played out. The light we see is not from the mist, that is gone too. It comes from the end of the tunnel."

Shar strained her eyes to see. Hope surged in her, for Asana was right. The mist was gone, but the light was growing and it was from outside.

They rushed ahead, clambering through a narrow way, at times crawling on hands and knees. Yet at length, they felt fresh air blow at them and the brightness was sharp like knives.

Soon, they came out into the light and stood, panting and ragged beneath the afternoon sun. They had no words, but a joy was upon them. The figure had not played them false. They were free, both of the enemy and the underground tunnels.

Turning around and looking, they soon discovered where they were.

"There is the sea," Asana said, pointing back the way they had come.

It looked beautiful to Shar. Here, they were higher above it than they had been in the village, and their vantage was from quite a distance.

"Over there," Kubodin said, and he pointed to the northwest. "That's the village."

Shar did not see it at first. They were high above it too, but it seemed far away. It was only like a dot in the distance, marked by a plume of smoke that rose up from it, bent and scattered quickly by the wind coming off the sea.

"We've come a long way," Nerchak said. "No wonder it took so long, but the nazram will never be able to follow us or guess where we went to."

Shar looked elsewhere. Mostly there was a forest, and few were the patches of grass. The ground was not level, and indeed they stood upon a tall hill, and others were all about them. It was a rugged land, and an easy one to hide in. She felt good for the first time since retrieving the

Swords of Dawn and Dusk. And the black figure, whoever or whatever it was, was responsible for that.

"Where has our guide gone?" she asked. For looking around, there was no sign of her.

"Whatever it was, I last saw it as we neared the cave mouth," Nerchak said.

No one had seen it after that, and Shar felt guilty for having doubted it. It had saved them.

"What do you think it was?" she asked.

Kubodin fingered his earring. "This is an old land, and there are old powers in it. It's said the gods still walk here openly. Maybe it was one of them."

Nerchak did not agree. "Have you ever seen such gods? I have heard sentiments like that in many lands, but no one has actually seen them. They just talk of them."

"Could be you're right," Kubodin replied. He did not seem to take offence. "But have you got a better explanation?"

Nerchak gave no answer to that. They all knew by now that whatever it was, it had not been human. At least, not a live person.

Shar turned to Asana. "What do you think?"

The swordmaster shrugged. "I don't know what to think. But does it matter? However it happened, we're here and have escaped the nazram. The why or the how is less important than the end result."

That was a typical answer for him. He seemed to just accept life as it came to him, the good or the bad. He was probably right to do so too, but something in this matter tugged away at Shar's mind, and she wanted to *know* what had happened. She felt it was important, but there was no way to find out. Perhaps, sometime in the future, the secret would be revealed.

She gazed out over the rugged landscape again, and looked forward to exploring the hills that marched away into the distance. Some of the tops of them were wreathed in an afternoon fog that seemed to flow down from the sky and settle there like little hats. If there was a fog there at this time of day, it would be thick by morning.

She took a breath. "You better lead us, Kubodin."

The little man hitched up his trousers. There was something different about him now, some look of determination and focus that had not been there before. He was in his own land now, or near it. He looked driven to achieve something, and he strode southward without another word.

They followed him in silence. All of them were deathly tired, and a rest would have served them well. Yet by a stroke of good fortune they had been delivered from the nazram, and that should not be squandered. It was best to get as far as possible from the village, and to do it as fast as possible.

Shar trudged along, covering the rear. There was no sign of anyone, but it was hard to tell. Swiftly they entered the thick forest, and it was dim beneath the evergreen trees. It was a forest of oaks, but there were many other varieties of trees as well, most of which Shar had no name for.

The dark grew deeper as they went, for not only did the forest continue to grow thicker but the sun was also lowering. They came to a rare clearing in the trees, and above the sky was visible. What clouds there were had a pink hue to them, a sign that the sun was setting or had even dipped below the rim of the world.

"Time to set camp," Asana recommended. "If we keep going much longer night will fall fast and we'll have no light."

No one argued. It had been the longest of days, and a meal and a night's rest beckoned them all.

"I think we can risk a fire," Shar said. "The trees will disperse the smoke and hide the flames from any prying eyes."

When they had eaten a meal and the fire had died down, they began to talk.

"Why do you hate the nazram so much?" Shar asked Kubodin. "Or why do they hate you?"

Kubodin sat bent down near the fire, but his hood was up and she could not see his face.

"They tried to kill me once. They nearly succeeded. And when I escaped, they hunted me like an animal. Again, they nearly killed me. Only the arrival of Asana saved me, and that was the first time we ever met."

That explained a lot to Shar. She knew Kubodin and Asana were the greatest of friends, but there was a loyalty there at the core of it that could not be broken. Now she knew why.

"Tell them why the nazram were trying to kill you," Asana suggested. "Everything stems from that."

Kubodin leaned back, and the hood moved, but his face was still in shadow.

"I am the son of a chieftain. The Two Ravens Clan is small, and it may seem a petty chieftainship to some, but not to us. Anyway, I was not the firstborn son, so thoughts of rule meant nothing to me. My older brother would inherit the responsibility, and I was more than content with that. And it was going to happen soon, for our father was gravely ill."

The little man spoke softly, and there was pain in his voice.

"Life was good to me, and the only sorrow was my father's illness. Yet one day, by chance, I discovered something terrible. My brother was poisoning him, for he did not wish to wait to assume the chieftainship. I had always thought he was rash and arrogant, but until then I had not known he was evil."

Shar felt a stab of sorrow at that. She could not imagine what Kubodin had gone through.

"I denounced my brother publicly, but I'm not sure that my father even understood what was happening. He was gravely ill by that time." Kubodin shook his head. "It was a rash decision, for my brother had a plan in case I discovered his secret. One that I suspect he had put much thought into and that he would have used in the end regardless of whether or not I knew the truth. He accused *me* of poisoning our father, and beginning to do the same to him. He produced the poison as evidence, which was convenient because he was the one who had it all along. But he claimed it was discovered in my hut."

The little man spoke quietly, and there was a hush to his words as though he was restraining himself from some great emotion. Little surprise, thought Shar, if he were.

"I won't tire you with the details. It's enough to say that the shaman Drasta supported him, and I was imprisoned. That was a pit in the ground with iron bars as a ceiling secured in stone. I spent three days in there, while my brother, Drasta, and the village council decided my fate. I knew it would be death because the council was under their sway and corrupt. My father had known it, and he had executed some for the crime when he was well. Something that must have spurred my brother into action, for I suspect he was corrupt also and my father's investigations, had they been allowed to continue, would have found him out."

Shar felt sick to the pit of her stomach, but Kubodin kept going in that matter-of-fact voice as though he were describing things that had happened to someone else.

"I was not without help though. No matter what my brother or the shaman said, most of the people knew better. They knew me and they knew my brother, and of the two of us they understood who would lie and who had the most to gain by doing so."

Kubodin shifted position, and Shar caught a gleam of his eyes. They were hard as stone.

"The details don't matter," the little man said. "But I was helped to escape, and my brother sent nazram after me. Drasta sent more. He summoned beasts of sorcery, and only my axe saved me from them. Yet at length I was caught. Caught and tortured. But before they killed me Asana happened by. That, my friends, is why the nazram hate me. I escaped, the only one of their victims to do so. I hate them more though. And my brother is yet to pay for the evil that he did. So too Drasta. For I believe that my brother was aided by him at all points, and that Drasta supplied the poison. Shamans know such things, though it's true that others do too."

It was a harrowing story, and after telling it Kubodin said he would take first watch. He wandered off into the night to be alone with his memories.

The others did not discuss it. They talked for a little while longer and then each lay down to find what rest they could. Shar found none though, and she tossed and turned and eventually rose and found Kubodin. He was not far from the camp, and his axe was in his hand and, as ever, he slowly sharpened it. Shar better understood why now. He never really sharpened the axe. Instead, he dreamed of revenge.

She took the watch then, and sitting down on a small boulder thrusting up from the ground she thought. Of poisons, her grandmother had taught her much. It was one of the many ways the shamans might try to kill her, and she had to know how to recognize them by taste and sight, as well as the remedies. At least when there was one.

The poisoning of Kubodin's father seemed obviously shaman's work to her, and it was just another evil to add to the long list of their misdeeds. Through history, Shulu had told her, thousands of officials and even quite a few chieftains had been so killed. All so that the shamans got their way in decisions.

Her heart hardened within her, and she was glad that she had come here. Helping Kubodin would be her own first strike in the war against the shamans that was coming.

11. Deeper into the Mists

The travelers struck camp at dawn and hastened southward, deeper into the Wahlum Hills.

It was a strange morning. During the night a dense fog formed, and now it was so thick that it was hard to see anything except the ground that lay close by. How Kubodin could find his way in this, Shar did not know.

But the little man walked with purpose and gave every impression he knew *exactly* where he was going. He probably did. Shar knew she could find her way in Tsarin Fen even if blindfolded, and it was much the same here. This was Kubodin's homeland, and he would know all its secrets.

The fog did not obscure vision alone, but also sound. There was a great hush over the land, and it was rarely broken except by the call of some distant bird.

They went on. The fog did not lessen as the day grew older, and the forests grew thicker still. Water dripped from the tips of leaves, and the trunks of the moss-covered trees were slick with moisture.

"This is Iron Dog territory," Kubodin said. "The Two Ravens Clan have been at war with them for centuries. Just now there is peace, at least there was when I left here. But it's better to travel in secrecy. Who knows what the mood is now? I don't even know about my own tribe. Much may have changed, and we need information first before we tell anyone who we are."

Shulu had told her little about the Iron Dogs, but Shar remembered what it was. As was so often the case, they and Kubodin's tribe were once one. Go back far enough in time, and all the Wahlum Hills were the territory of a single king.

The Iron Dogs had a reputation for being wild and fearless. Maybe even cruel. Then again, it was a hard land. If the rest of the Cheng suffered, those in the Wahlum Hills suffered more. Poverty was everywhere, and many children died from malnutrition and disease. Despite all this, they had a reputation for loyalty, once it was earned, and a spirit of fairness.

There were multiple tribes in the hills, and Shar thought through them. What applied to the Iron Dogs applied to the rest as well. They warred among each other with frequency, but they were fundamentally the one clan divided into smaller, and feuding, family units.

So Shulu had instructed her. She had never said where the Iron Dogs got their name from though. It was an unusual one, even in a land where clan names were often strange.

"I don't like this fog," Nerchak muttered as they walked. "We could step straight into a trap and never notice it until it closed on us."

He was right. Nor did the fog seem to change much. It was thicker when they passed into one of the many small valleys between the hills, but even the heights were covered by it.

Yet as the hours drew on eventually the white glow of the sun through the vapor could be seen, and by noon most of it had been burned away. Only tattered remnants remained on the slopes of the highest hills, but they too soon faded from sight.

The company stopped for lunch. Kubodin chose the crest of the hill, and after they had eaten he climbed a tree and looked out over the land in all directions.

"What do you see?" Asana asked.

"Trees," came the reply.

The swordmaster did not seem annoyed by the answer. Rather, he smiled.

"Anything else?"

"Hills."

Asana nodded gravely. "Yes. And the sky as well?"

Kubodin clambered down the trunk. "You're smarter than you look. Yes. Lots of sky." He flashed a grin at his friend. "But no sign of anyone else. Still, that doesn't mean a lot. An army could hide in some of those forested valleys and not be seen for weeks."

They went ahead after that, traveling quietly and avoiding all trails, of which there were many though most seemed old and unused.

After a time, Kubodin told them how the tribes were organized in the hills.

"Near the coast," he said, "is the Swimming Osprey Clan. They rarely leave the northern coastline and come inland except for certain years where the tribes gather and tell the ancient stories in peace. That happens seldom."

He pointed around them as they walked. "As you know, this is Iron Dog land, and they're great hunters and fair fighters. Soon, we'll reach my Two Ravens Tribe. We're the best fighters in the hills. No doubt about that." He winked at Shar. "And we have the most handsome men in all the hills. But you know that already."

Shar suppressed her smile and ignored him, but he went on undisturbed.

"Beyond my tribe, which encompasses the middle parts of the hills, there are the Smoking Eyes Clan and the Running Bear Clan. Those are good fighters too."

Shar had not heard of them. She guessed they were small tribes. Certainly, the way she understood it, the Two Ravens Clan was the biggest and most influential in the area. They all warred against each other at times, but they respected each other too, and the Two Ravens were seen as the older brother of the area and their chief sometimes settled disputes between the others. This was different than most areas of the old Cheng Empire, for the shamans had less power here.

They spent another night in the fog-shrouded hills, and as dusk fell drums began to beat, wild and haunting. It stirred something in Kubodin, and his eyes gleamed in the faint light of the small fire.

Shar tried to determine where the noise came from, but she could not. The folds of the land were too many, the forests too thick and the fog too dense. She had no idea if they were close by or far away. And when one drum ceased to beat another would start from an entirely different direction. So it went on, like some strange game.

"They speak to each other," Kubodin said.

Shar sensed emotion in his voice. "What do they say?"

"Some say, *We are the Two Ravens Clan.*"

"And the others?"

"They answer, *We are the Iron Dogs. Beware!*"

"Does that mean they're in conflict?"

Kubodin scratched his head. "Not really. The beating of those drums has gone on every night for near on a thousand years. Sometimes there's more than drum beats though. The young warriors on either side can get excited to prove themselves, and war cries sound as well."

Shar was not comforted by that answer. It sounded to her like the young warriors might prowl the borderlands between the tribes, and that was right where she and her companions were now. It made her peer out into the dark, but she could see nothing.

They slept, keeping turns as usual now to maintain a watch. All night the drums continued, sullen and moody, like the wild heartbeat of the hills themselves.

Dawn came swiftly, and for once there seemed little fog. The travelers began to move again, and Kubodin led them along silent trails, always moving slowly. At various times they found fresh tracks, and they knew that someone had been near their camp last night, but might not have known it was there after the fire died down.

"Keep your eyes open, and don't even blink," Kubodin warned them. "Hill men of any tribe are expert at hiding in this country. And they might be inclined to attack first and talk later."

So they went, carefully and slowly, and fear was on them of being discovered. Shar was not sure if it would be worse if it were Two Ravens warriors or Iron Dogs who discovered them. But despite seeing many more tracks and knowing that those who played the drums last night must live in villages close by, they saw no one.

After climbing a steep hill they descended into an equally steep valley. It was lush with growth, and the trees were gnarled and thick trunked. If the hills were old, it seemed to Shar that this was an ancient forest untouched by human hands. There was something almost mystical about it, as though the gods of the Wahlum Hills dwelled here.

But it was not as untouched as it seemed. Even here there was a trail, though it was a game trail and likely frequented by deer. Yet still Kubodin silently pointed at some marks as they walked, and though he said nothing Shar recognized the scuff of a boot in the loamy soil as readily as he did.

They reached the bottom of the valley, and a narrow stream ran through it. This they crossed merely by stepping over it, but no doubt in times of rain it would widen greatly for the land was flat here and there were signs of past floods.

They came to the other side, and there Kubodin suddenly stopped. He made no move. He barely seemed to breathe, and the others copied him, not knowing why but sure that if Kubodin was wary there was a good reason for it.

"I know you're there," Kubodin said. "Behind the big oak. Come out. This is no war band, and we're friendly. At least, we will be if you are."

There was silence. Nothing moved. But after a few moments a man stepped out from behind the tree, and he could have been Kubodin himself.

He had the same look to him, even wearing much the same clothes. All that was different was that he carried no axe but had a short yet heavy-bladed sword sheathed at his side. He even spoke like Kubodin.

"What's all the fuss? Can't a man hunt anymore without being invited to talk to every passerby?"

For all that he spoke in such a relaxed manner, as though he knew them all, his hand was close to the hilt of that sword and his gaze was sharp.

"We'll leave you in peace," Kubodin answered. He would have noticed, as Shar had, that the man carried no bow and was a warrior rather than a hunter. But he did not mention it. "Since we've disturbed you, maybe you could give us the news of the land? I'm returning from far away."

The warrior looked him up and down. "You're Two Ravens. No doubt about that. What are you doing with *them*?" As he spoke, he gestured at the others with his thumb.

"They're friends. Good friends, and I vouch for them in the land where our ancestors made the first trails."

Shar was not sure what that last bit meant. It obviously had some sort of significance though, for the warrior, though barely showing any outward sign, was suddenly relaxed.

"You must have traveled long and far not to know what's going on here. It's all bad. But when hasn't it been?"

"A good point. It's been going from bad to worse for a thousand years."

Shar nearly missed the import of that, but Kubodin was trying to get a feel for how this man thought of the emperor, or if he preferred the shamans. He got a swift answer.

The warrior grimaced. "A dangerous thing to say these days. True though."

Kubodin nodded. "These are dangerous times. Does Kuthondrin still rule?"

The other man looked at him sharply. "He does. Drasta aids him, and the council of elders still support him despite all he's done. But you'd know all about that, Kubodin."

Kubodin laughed, but it was a grim sound. "True enough. But it's time for old wrongs to be righted, Radatan. When did you recognize me?"

"I knew you for a warrior when you spoke of the ancestral trails. That password has changed now, though. For the last year the phrase to identify one another has been to mention Kuthondrin's axe. But I only knew you when you mentioned the chief's name. Then I remembered why you seemed so familiar. We only met the once though, and it was long ago."

"I remember. You really are a hunter, and you guided my father once to some wild boar in a deep valley to the north."

The other man looked impressed. "I'm surprised you remembered that. You should know though, warrior to warrior, that it's dangerous for you here. Your brother still rules with an iron grip, and he'll kill you if he can. Word is he still rants about how you escaped when he gets drunk."

Kubodin laughed. "Well, you just made my day! I'm glad that I've got under his skin, but I'll do more yet before this is over. Tell me about his axe though. He never used to wield one."

Radatan glanced at Kubodin's own axe, looped through his belt.

"He pretends it's that one. Says it should have been his, and now those close to him say he really does think the new one Drasta made for him is the original."

"This is one of a kind," Kubodin said, but Shar noticed him glance at her own swords and she remembered the voices that rang out of swords and axes alike in Chatchek Fortress. They were not unique, for Shulu had made several such items. The others though were likely lost over such a long time.

"Anyway," Kubodin said, "thank you for your time Radatan. Best not to mention to anyone that I'm back yet."

Radatan bowed, gave a searching look over all the others as though he wondered who they were but decided it was better not to ask, and then faded away into the trees with great skill. In just a few moments Shar had completely lost sight of him, nor did he make any sound.

"A good bit of luck that you knew and trusted him," Asana said when the hunter was gone.

"Luck, maybe. Or just the favor of the gods, perhaps. They do like me, I'm told."

"Something was working for you," Shar added. "Did you learn anything though?"

"I did. He didn't mention that anyone was searching for me, so likely Drasta thought the nazram would take care of me. That was an error of judgement."

Shar thought of something else. "Nor did he mention that the emperor's swords had been found, or that anyone was searching for me."

"No. That was good news too. Of my coming here, Drasta somehow knew. But he has no idea who I'm with."

After the meeting with Radatan, Kubodin led them deeper into the mists. Shar had thought Tsarin Fen was wild and isolated, but this land was like some fragment of the ancient world living on into modern times. Armies could come here to conquer, and end up disappearing from the earth, never to be seen again.

She began to fear that a warrior stood behind each tree, and that her enemies knew of her coming and lured her into a trap. If an army could disappear here, so too could she. A grave was calling to her, shallow beneath the rotting leaves, and the wolves would gnaw on her forgotten bones.

It was no way to live, but fear would be her companion until she had gathered an army. First, to protect herself. And then to take the fight to her adversaries and the enemies of freedom.

But first they must deal with Kubodin's brother and the shaman Drasta. It seemed clear that one or both of them had decided to keep their knowledge of Kubodin's return secret. Small wonder, for if news of that passed around then there would be great unrest. It was a mistake though.

What they should have done instead was to revive all the old stories and circulate the lie that he had killed his own father. That would have weakened support for Kubodin if he returned.

Yet they had sought to keep it secret and kill him away from home. Now, when he returned, likely before knowledge came to Drasta or the chief that their plan had failed, he would arrive with tremendous surprise. If he could harness that and turn it to his advantage he might overthrow the tyrant that was his brother before a plan could be put in place to stop him.

Shar walked ahead, and it worried her that she could so easily follow the plans and schemes of her enemies and find the flaws in them. If she could do that, then she could scheme herself.

And she would need to in order to live. That worried her even more. Who would the Shar of the future be, if she survived to become emperor?

12. The Black Fox

The nazram regathered in a farmer's field outside the seaside village where they had lost their prey.

Shunwahrin fumed, but he did so silently while he waited for all his men to return. It would not do to show his anger, or even worse, reveal his doubts to the men. A leader must be in control at all times, especially during those times when he was not.

He was not now. The reports kept coming in that their quarry had disappeared. Worse, after questioning villagers, it had been discovered that there had been multiple sightings in different streets all going in different directions. They had been seen in the north, south, east and west of the city at the same time.

It reeked to him of magic. Kubodin was said to have some skill in the arts of the shamans. Shunwahrin had never believed that rumor, but he did now. Or else it was one of the fugitive's companions.

Drasta had not mentioned that Kubodin would be accompanied. One of those companions was strange too. Some of his men had reported hearing a female voice warn Kubodin. Others said that she was a spirit that floated through walls. Some had not seen her at all, and this seemed the most probable truth.

Yet Shunwahrin had learned there were many strange things in the world, and it was some of his best men that had sworn they had seen her.

The last of his men trudged into the field as dusk settled over the land.

"Did you find anything?" he asked.

"Nothing. There were tracks on the beach, but we couldn't identify who made them. The villagers nearby had seen no one."

Shunwahrin dismissed them. It was not the first report of tracks on the beach, but like the sightings themselves it seemed there were tracks everywhere.

It did not matter. He had been thwarted, but he had a remedy for that.

He gave orders to establish a camp. They would stay here for the night, and the next morning they would head back toward Two Ravens land. That was where Kubodin would head.

Fires were started, and the men sat around them as night fell. They were subdued, and well they might be. Like a fisherman who drew his net up from the sea with a large catch in it, the fish had somehow slipped out of the net before being brought into the boat. The nazram had been made fools of, but that would not work to Kubodin's favor. The men would be harsher with him when they found him, and that made Shunwahrin smile for the first time that day.

But find him they must, and as soon as possible. It should not be difficult. Drasta had given him a means to do so, but it was only to be used as a last resort.

Night fell, and he waited for the camp to go quiet before he acted. He rose from the fire he sat before, and told his second in command to stay where he was. Then he walked toward the perimeter. He was challenged by a sentry, as he should have been, but the man bowed and backed away when he saw who it was.

Shunwahrin walked into the night and away from his men. The field he trod had been planted to wheat, and thanks to his men much of it had been trampled into dust. The farmer would not be happy about that, but he had stayed in his cottage all day and said nothing. Just as well, for he would have been killed had he complained. His field was as nothing compared to the welfare of the tribe.

There was a hedge ahead, and Shunwahrin passed through it. No one would have dared followed him, but the magic he possessed was not for other eyes. He wanted privacy for this.

On the other side of the hedge was a boulder, and from here he could see the lights of the village twinkling some way away. He looked around to make certain he was alone, and then he drew out an item from his pocket.

It was cold to touch. He could barely see it, for it was black. Jade, Drasta had called it. Shunwahrin had never seen that precious stone before, but he had heard of it. The shamans liked it and used it for many things.

He held the object in his hand, and traced its outline with his fingers. It was a whistle. It was supposed to make a strange sound, and it was said that in days of old such devices were used to send a signal that carried above the din of battle and gave commands to warriors when even the shouting of a captain might not carry to them.

He held it to his lips as Drasta had shown him, but hesitated to blow. He did not trust the shaman. The man was a snake, and this was no ordinary whistle but a talisman of magic. And magic often had unintended consequences. Still, if something happened to him he would not be able to fulfil his charge of finding and killing Kubodin. So he should be safe.

He blew the whistle, and a strange sound, high pitched like the screaming of a rabbit came from it. He took a breath, and blew again, only louder this time. Then he did so once more. Three times he had been instructed to blow, and then to wait.

He put the object back in his pocket. He knew what would answer his call, and he did not like it. Yet still, every creature on the earth served its purpose.

The night was dark. The stars in the sky seemed dim, and from far away he heard the ceaseless sound of the ocean murmur restlessly.

He waited. And out of the dark a figure emerged. She came warily at first, almost scenting the air for signs of danger or a trap. But she came on, one cautious step at a time, circling in on him rather than walking in a straight line.

She was beautiful. That much he could see as she came closer. A slight woman, yet with long black hair that trailed out behind her and fell to her waist. Of her eyes, he could see little, but they seemed to gleam with the light of the stars.

Several times he thought she would turn and flee, but ever she came on, and the closer she got the bolder she became. She sensed there was no danger here.

"You summoned me?" she asked. And her voice held a wild beauty in it. Shunwahrin had been warned what to expect, but not about this.

The woman smiled at him, and her teeth caught the glimmer of starlight even as her eyes had done.

"Don't be shy. Come! Speak to me. Tell me what you wish, and I will serve."

Shunwahrin straightened. The whistle felt cold as ice in his hand, but he ignored it.

"There is one called Kubodin. I seek him. He—"

"I know who he is." The lady stood very close to him now, and the long shadow that was her black hair brushed against his body. He remained still, as though turned to ice, but she laughed.

"Why so formal? Are we not friends? I know all about Kubodin, but I would rather know about you."

Shunwahrin took a step back. "Kubodin is all that matters. He has escaped. He will be heading toward Two Ravens land, and you must find him. Find him, and tell me where he is. I will be heading back that way too, as fast as I can travel with the nazram."

The black-haired lady eyed him for a moment, and then she laughed and leaped nimbly to the top of the boulder. Once there, she sat down with grace and studied him.

"Yes, yes, yes. I can find Kubodin for you. Nothing easier. I can scent a trail that no tracker could ever find. But what then?"

"Then I will kill him."

Her eyes gleamed at that. "There is nothing like the thrill of the hunt. But what then? What about you and me?"

He took another step away from her. She was a creature of magic and beguilement. He knew he meant nothing to her, and this was but a game in her eyes.

She studied him closely. "You're no fun. No fun at all."

"I'm a nazram. I *lead* the nazram. Nothing we do is for fun. All we do is for the shamans."

She rolled her eyes at him. "Such a warrior answer. Even the shamans know how to have more fun than you do."

Her gaze lingered on him a little while longer, then with fluid grace she gathered her legs under herself and leaped off the boulder, her black hair shadowing the air in her wake.

Yet she landed softly, and her form had changed in that smooth movement. She was not a lady anymore but had transformed, like the shapeshifter she was, into a fox. Nor any fox, but a black fox, dark as midnight and with a long and luxurious tail. The night swallowed her in a moment, and she was gone.

The legends of such creatures among the Cheng were numerous, but Shunwahrin had not seen one before. It was a creature such as this who had once tried to beguile the emperor and kill him. Only she had been killed instead.

Kubodin was no emperor though. He did not possess magic swords, and she need not kill him. No. All she had to do was find him and report back, and the nazram would do the job they had been sent to do.

13. A Sign of Luck

The travelers followed a narrow ridge that ran up the side of a tall hill, and then they swung around due south. There, they stopped.

If it were a mountain trail, this would be a pass. There was another hill on their left, and they stood between the two like a small party of humans flanked by giants. Each hill had broad shoulders, then a narrow neck that was topped by a prominence like a head. Yet they were not man shaped. From each thrust out a ledge, and though not uniform or of the exact same size, they were of solid rock and bereft of trees. They looked like the beaks of birds, and suddenly Shar understood why Kubodin's tribe took the name of the Two Ravens Clan.

The ravens did not look toward the pass. Their gazes were turned toward the valley below, for there was a vast one that ran crosswise to the hills, and it was lush with massive trees rising above the mist-filled lower airs. Where Shar could see the ground, she saw some open fields where herds were gathered and crops grown. There were several small rivers, but mostly there were trees, tall and profuse. It was a lush valley, watered well by hills all around. It was beautiful too, and she turned her gaze to Kubodin and was surprised to see tears in his eyes.

The little hill man surprised her more. He went down upon his knees, and he touched the ground with his hands.

"This," he told them, "is my home. My true home. We have passed through the lands of my clan for some while, but this valley is the spiritual birthplace of the Two Ravens. This is where our great ancestor was born, our first chief. This is our sacred land, and above us on the tops of each hill the rites are held for the initiation of men and woman into adulthood, and on those outthrusts of rock all our chiefs must walk, where no others are allowed and few would dare to go, and there they are initiated into their rulership."

He was silent a moment. Then he spoke again, almost to himself.

"These are the lands my forefathers trod. These are the lands my foremothers knew. Here I was born, and to here I return, bringing justice with me if life and blood will serve."

Then he stood, hitched his trousers higher, and was the old Kubodin once more that Shar knew.

"We're here," she said. "But where to now? Have you got a plan?"

He turned and smiled at her, but there was still a sheen of tears in his eyes.

"Have I got a plan? Are hills hard to climb? Of course I have a plan. And a brilliant one."

"What is it, then?" Asana asked.

The little man shrugged. "My plan is to make it up as I go. That's always worked well for me in the past."

He did not wait for any reply. Instead, he led them down the trail into the valley. It was the best worn trail they had seen so far, and it was the only one leading where they wished to go, so they had to follow it. Yet Kubodin pulled his hood up in case they ran into anyone, and at the first opportunity some half a mile later he took a narrow path that veered away to the left.

They saw no one, however. The scent of smoke was strong in the air though, and there were no doubt multiple villages not that far away.

"Are you really making this up as you go?" Shar asked him.

He stepped over a log that had fallen across the path, and answered as he held her hand to assist her over it in her turn.

"Not really. I have many friends here, unless things have changed. Maybe more now than when I left, for the people will have been ground under my brother's heel and have had a chance to know him better. It will only take word of my return to spread, and I'll have an army of supporters."

Shar considered that as they continued along the dim trail overhung by the branches of tall trees.

"You go to see someone in particular. Someone who you can trust to spread that word, but in secret to your followers first and not your opposition. That way you hope to use surprise to your advantage."

He almost seemed surprised. "Exactly. Shulu Gan really did teach you, didn't she?"

Shar did not answer as they kept walking. She missed her grandmother, and she even missed all those hard lessons. Sword fighting. Politics. Negotiation. History. Dar Shun and medicine. When the mood was on her, Shulu had taken their training into any one of a thousand different fields of study.

It was dark beneath the trees, and there were few clearings. Yet always the scent of smoke was in the air, and even at times they heard people in the distance.

They met no one on the trail. Perhaps they were just lucky, but Kubodin seemed to sense when there was someone nearby, and he took them for a while into the thick stands of trees to wait in silence before returning back to the path. Or taking a different one, for the deeper into the valley they traveled the more paths there were.

Toward the afternoon they reached flatter ground. The forest, if anything, was thicker and taller. But they came to a ford across one of the many streams, and that was in the open.

Kubodin waited several minutes. He was never in any hurry, and less so now. Night was coming, and it would give them cover as they neared the most populated areas.

Satisfied at last, he led them forward. He stopped halfway across the ford though, with the water lapping at his calves.

Shar saw why. It was no person, but a bird. A raven, larger than any she had ever seen and glossy black, floated down from somewhere in the forest to land gracefully on the dead stump of a tree to the side of the ford. It flicked its wings, fixed them with a sideways glance of its eye for a moment, then gave its typical gurgling croak and flew away with its characteristic cumbersome grace.

Kubodin did not take his gaze off it until it disappeared within the forest.

"A good sign!" he muttered. "The raven is my totem."

Shar did not believe in such things, but had she seen a fen wolf right now she knew her spirit would have soared too.

They moved carefully through the thick forest, and Kubodin had many paths to choose from now. Always he chose the smallest and less traveled one, even if it meant taking a far longer route to where he was going.

Mostly, they kept away from the streams, for it was along their banks that many villages were established. Yet the time came when the trees started to give way to large clearings, and the bellowing of cattle and the bleating of sheep were common. The largest villages of the Two Ravens Clan were close now.

It seemed strange to Shar that there were so many villages here, but close together. In the fens it was different. The populace was more spread out and villages were often distant. But this was a smaller land, and the abundance of good soil and fresh water drew the people close together. Their lands extended beyond this one valley, but here, as Kubodin had said, was their true home.

They came to a stop beneath a stand of tall oaks. There was a fringe of ferns growing in the half light, and then open ground grazed by a small and wild looking breed of cattle.

Beyond the fields a village lay, and it was quite large. A river ran close to it, and the flat lands to each side were cultivated and plentiful with crops and orchards. Smoke rose from many of the huts, and it seemed a peaceful land.

"We'll wait for night," Kubodin told them. "We can go no farther now without being seen, and I'm not ready for that just yet."

They rested under the cover of trees as the sun lowered and afternoon shadows lengthened. Dusk fell quickly, for the surrounding rim of hills blocked it out sooner than would otherwise have been.

"Best to eat something now," Kubodin advised. "We can risk no fire here for light later on."

They ate a cold meal, and Shar did not like it. She hated hiding and skulking, but necessity demanded it just now. So too it demanded a sentry at all times, and they took turns keeping watch. They were so close to people now that there was a great risk of being discovered.

Yet Kubodin had chosen his place of concealment well, and no one came this way.

Time passed slowly, and when night fell they watched lights spring to life in the village and even smelled food cooking. Kubodin made no move though. Not yet.

Shar would have done the same. It was still too early, and if they went down to the village now there would always be the chance of running into someone on the narrow roads between the rows of huts. It would be better to wait until much later in the night when everyone was in their own home and preparing for sleep.

Fog rolled down from the surrounding hills, and mists rose from the streams to spread out tendrils to meet it. They waited, resting in the quiet of the night, and despite the peace feeling fear rising in them.

It was one thing for Kubodin to return home and try to claim the chieftainship, but it was another to succeed. His brother had outmaneuvered him once, and his brother still retained the threads of power in his hands. He had a shaman to call upon, and the council of elders, and the nazram and warriors. What did Kubodin have?

But that, Shar knew. He had the truth, which was a great power if it came to light. And, it might be, the will of more than half the people. No chief nor shaman could suppress a people unless they allowed it.

Shar watched an owl in the tree nearby glide to a branch farther away. Then another joined it, flying silent and smooth. Then by turns three more, small and less graceful. It was a new family of them, and this was one of their first flights. They hopped and hovered, changing position and playing. Then, again by turns, they flew into a higher branch and were gone from sight.

Kubodin stirred. "Time to go," he said, and his voice was subdued. He too felt the weight of responsibility for the events he was about to set in motion.

For Kubodin, it might be death if he failed. For the rest of them, they would suffer the same fate unless they abandoned him. That, they would never do. For Shar though, it was a surer death than even Kubodin.

Kubodin would help her though, if he became chief. But how much? Was it possible that he was using her to help gain the chieftainship? She could not dismiss that chance. Without doubt, she was a kind of weapon for him. By bringing her here, it would help sway his people to rebellion against his brother and the shaman. He could use her as a kind of token, showing that fate was on his side, and that the gods favored his cause.

The more these hill people disliked the shamans, the more that would prove true. And from what Shulu had told her, and from what she had begun to see herself, these hill tribes were very independent. They might be quick to overthrow the rule of their shamans, but they might not be so quick to just cede power to a new authority that was not one of them and only had a *claim* to be the emperor's heir. Even her great forefather had trouble controlling the tribes when he *was* the actual emperor.

They moved across open land now, but the dark and the creeping mists obscured them. So too, there should be few people about to see them even if they could, for the night was getting old now, and the middle reaches of it were close.

In the distance, Shar heard the gurgle of the stream, and the gathering of huts bulked up now in the shadows. The village was even bigger than it looked from farther away.

They slipped into it and walked the shadows of its lanes. Now and then a dog barked at them. From time to time the light of a fire could be seen in a hearth, but they ran into no people.

Kubodin led them through the village, and he came to a hut near the center. There he waited a while, watching to see if anyone was near. In the hut he faced, light escaped through the cracks around the door. It was faint though, and it did not mean anyone was still awake.

"I may be wrong," he whispered. "The one who lived here was a great friend, but it may be that they are dead now. Or moved elsewhere. Or maybe their heart has changed over the years. I don't know, but this is a moment of danger. Beware."

The little man placed one hand on the handle of his axe, and with the other he knocked softly on the door. It was a peculiar knock, with a rhythm to it, and Shar was certain that this was not the first time he had knocked on that door, and that the one inside had once known him very well. If she still lived there.

14. Rumor

All was silent, and Kubodin did not knock again. Shar feared the occupant was asleep, but then a noise came from inside.

The travelers stepped back a little way from the door, and all of them kept their hands close to their weapons.

There was more fumbling and a muttered curse. The light seeping out from the cracks around the door grew brighter as though more wood had been thrown on the dying fire. Then the door opened, not slowly and cautiously but fast and all the way.

Shar had been wrong. This was no woman here, but a warrior. He was bare chested, and even in the dim light she could see scars etched over his body and along his arms. In one hand was a sword, and it was raised. It mattered nothing that this was an old man, for she saw now that his hair was white and his back a little bent. Even so, there was strength in his arms and skill in the way he held the blade.

The old warrior filled the doorway, and by opening it fully he had given himself room to fight, if that was called for. But he did not attack. He stood ready, but he held his ground and peered at the group confronting him.

If the warrior were bemused, even anxious at having strangers knock on his door in the middle of the night, Shar did not blame him. And he did look bemused as his gaze swept over them all, but it lingered on Kubodin.

The old man took a step forward and peered at the little hill man.

"Is that you, Kubi?"

It seemed strange to Shar that the fierce warrior she knew had a nickname such as that, but this was a man who might have known him in his childhood.

"Ah," Kubodin said. "It's good to be recognized. Looks like you haven't gone senile yet, hey?"

The old man straightened and he slowly lowered his sword.

"Not yet, boy." He looked around to see if there was anyone else. "You better come inside. It's not safe for you out there."

He went inside himself and threw the sword down on his bed. It was nothing more than some thick blankets on the dirt floor. The travelers followed him, and Shar came in last, shutting the door behind her after a final look to see that they were not watched.

The old man put some more timber on the fire, and it blazed up with smoke and light.

"And how are you, Namarlin?" Kubodin asked.

"Old, and too tired to be woken in the middle of the night."

"Aren't you glad to see me?"

The old man finished throwing wood on the fire and straightened slowly.

"You've always been trouble, boy. But I've missed you. We all have these last few years."

Then to Shar's surprise the old man hugged Kubodin fiercely.

"Come! Sit!" he said.

There were no chairs, but the old man sat on his bed and handed over rugs for the others to use.

"Who are your friends?" the old warrior asked.

"You will have heard of Asana?" Kubodin said, gesturing at the swordmaster.

"Very pleased to meet you, Namarlin."

The old man raised his eyebrows. "I'm humbled, Asana Gan. This poor hut has never hosted a more famous warrior."

"My reputation is exaggerated," Asana replied. "Thank you for welcoming me."

The old man rubbed his face. "Exaggerated, is it? I doubt it. More likely you've done more than the stories say. But you're not the type, I think, to admit that."

"This is Nerchak," Kubodin said next, introducing the young warrior.

"Pleased to meet you," the old man said.

Kubodin then glanced at Shar, and he nodded slightly to her. She knew what it meant. If she wished, she could reveal her true identity. Kubodin trusted this man.

"And this," Kubodin said, "is a great friend to me."

He did not name her, leaving the choice as hers alone. She bowed her head and thought quickly. Her hood was up, and it was a little too dark for the man to have noticed her eyes. She could keep it that way, or she could place her trust in Kubodin.

She raised her head and let her hood fall back. There was silence a moment, and then the old man hissed through his teeth as he noticed her violet eyes.

"I am Shar," she proclaimed, 'heir to the emperor. But tonight, I'm but a humble guest in your home, and I thank you for your hospitality."

The old man was shocked, but like the warrior he was he recovered quickly. Bowing deeply from his seated position, he answered.

"You are welcome, lady. Now, and always." He glanced then at Kubodin. "You keep yourself in esteemed company, boy."

Kubodin grinned, but said nothing. The old man studied them all carefully.

"I heard a rumor yesterday," he said, "that the nazram across all the tribes are mobilized. They search for a woman who carries two swords. But that knowledge is not widespread yet."

Shar stood up. "The shamans would rather keep quiet that I exist. All the more so that I have the swords. I'll cause them great problems if I can. Just my existence alone is enough to threaten them." She drew her two blades with a flourish, and they glinted in the ruddy light of the fire. "But you know the truth, and I trust you with it for Kubodin's sake."

The old man watched her, and his face was unreadable. Then it broke out in a smile.

"I think you'll give them hell. You have that look about you, but your secret is safe with me until you want it known."

Namarlin got up and poured water into a pot which he put over the fire. Then he took some crushed leaves from a pouch and put them into the pot as well.

"Since we look like we're going to talk for a while, we may as well have something warm to drink."

They discussed small matters while the dried herbs infused into the water, then the old man poured them each a drink. He glanced at Kubodin's axe when the little man drew it out of his belt to sit more comfortably.

"Beware of that thing, boy. Your father told me its secrets one day. At least as far as he knew or guessed them. It's a weapon with two edges, and I don't mean just the blades."

"You knew Kubodin's father?" Shar asked.

The old man laughed. "Knew him? We were best of friends. I miss him still, but in our youth we were never apart. Feasts, battles, hunting, it didn't matter. We were always together. If there's any mercy to all this, at least he didn't know what Kuthondrin did to him."

"Kuthondrin is my brother," Kubodin explained.

"Do they all know the story?" the old man asked.

Kubodin nodded. "I've told them. But that's old news now. Tell me how my brother rules, and how the people feel about it."

The old man sighed. "Your brother wasn't always bad. At least, he didn't seem so as a child. Things are bad now though. Not long after you escaped, I was cast off the council of elders. They were always a nest of vipers, but they're your brother's men now, each and every one of them. They grow wealthy off his decisions, and he bribes them in many ways. They'll not support you."

"And what of Drasta?" Kubodin asked.

"Him? That snake is still alive, and he's the most venomous of them all. He stews in his own vitriol that one, scheming up ways to get out of these hills and to gather more power than a hill tribe can give him. But the other shamans either fear him or think him a fool. They never agree to letting him leave here. He'll support your brother, no doubt about that."

"No wonders there," Kubodin said. "What about the warriors and the people themselves?"

Shar leaned forward, interested in what the old man would say about that. Not only Kubodin's future rested on the answer, but in no small part her own.

"Well, that's straight to the heart of what really matters. After you escaped, word spread of your claims and many believed it. They look at Kuthondrin and see him for what he is. They want no part of him, but at the same time to resist would be to divide the clan in war. Without you here, no one was willing to do that. You are the only other heir."

"And how many," Kubodin asked, "do you think would fight for me now that I've returned?"

The old man ran a sinewy hand through his sparse hair and thought on the question.

"Impossible to say, my boy. You were always well liked, and apart from the story of your father's death your brother has made many mistakes and many enemies. He enriches himself and his allies, and the people suffer. They know it, but picking up a sword and fighting is a lot harder than speaking out among friendly ears where the nazram can't hear."

There was a lull in the conversation after that. They sipped their drinks and Kubodin thought.

"I've made up my mind," the little man said. "This isn't about trying to claim the chieftainship. It's about justice for my father, and about offering the people a choice. I *will* try to topple my brother. He's a murderer, and he's abused his power. What will happen after that, no man knows. But if truth and courage can win out, I'll exile him and rule as my father would have done."

Outside there was a patter of rain on the straw roof, but it soon passed. "Will you help me?" Kubodin asked.

Namarlin rested his hand over Kubodin's. "I will. For your sake. For your father's sake. And for the Two Ravens people. But the road ahead is dark, and I fear much blood will be spilled before we come to the light again."

"I fear that also," Kubodin said.

Outside the rain came again, only louder this time. Shar usually loved it, but not just now. She did not think they would spend the night under cover of this roof.

She knew exactly what she would do if she were Kubodin, and it would not involve staying here. It was too risky. If his brother somehow discovered him, he could be surrounded and overpowered. No. He would need to go somewhere else. He would need a lair where he could hide, and one that he could defend or retreat from at his choice. Most of all, he would need a place from which he could watch the land and gather tidings and see what the enemy was doing.

The rain pounded down louder, and Shar knew that soon she would be walking through it.

15. The Oath Stone

It was growing warm in the hut, and the travelers had finished their leaf-infused water.

"I'll do all I can to aid you, Kubi," Namarlin said. "I'm an old man, and death gets closer every day. I've nothing to lose, but you … you had better be careful."

"I will be. I know I never looked it, but I've always been cautious. Under the influence of Asana, I'm even more so now. This will be a bad time, but we'll come out the other side of it."

The old man appraised him. "You *have* grown up. What will be will be, though. In the meantime, tell me what you want me to do."

Kubodin did not hesitate. He had already thought this through.

"Get word to those who'll rally to my call. Start tonight, and be careful who you tell, and tell them to be careful who they tell in turn, in both this village and the surrounding ones. Let them bring their swords or spears, and their courage too. Get them to rally at the Oath Stone."

"You know," Namarlin replied, "that word will get to your brother. Someone will say the wrong thing to the wrong person. He'll know your plan."

"Of course. It cannot be kept a secret, but he'll need time to rally his own forces, and if I can get even just a few hours head start on him the advantage will be mine."

Shar was not so sure of that. The plan was a gamble, but it always would be.

They left soon after. The rain had died down to a soft drizzle, and they said goodbye to the old man. He came out with them, wrapping his cloak tightly about him and pulling up his hood. He and Kubodin embraced, then they shook hands.

A few moments later the old man had headed off in one direction, and Kubodin led the travelers the opposite way. It was dark in the village, and few were the lights now in any house. Namarlin would get a poor reception at whoever's door he knocked on, but hopefully that mood would change when they heard that Kubodin had returned.

They left the village behind them, and they moved northward, back in the direction they had come from, but not to the same place.

"What's the Oath Stone?" Shar asked once they were out of earshot of the village and there was little chance of being heard or seen.

"It's an old place, and a sacred one in this valley that is sacred itself." He led them over a tiny brook that bubbled across their path, but they could clear it simply by jumping. "It existed in the emperor's time, though its uses before then have been somewhat forgotten. We know it was used, even as it is now, for marriages and other binding promises. It was there also that your great forefather accepted the pledge of loyalty from our people."

Shar was surprised at that. "You mean he was here?"

"Of course! He came to all the tribes, either in war or in peace. With us, it was in peace. We readily accepted him, and in token of that we cast out the shamans from the land."

It was not something that Shar had expected. As at Chatchek fortress, she would stand in the very place that her ancestor had once stood. It seemed that she followed in his footsteps, and there was something reassuring in that. For the most part, anyway. In the end he had been betrayed and murdered.

"When the shamans came back, why didn't they destroy the stone like they did with so many other things the emperor was associated with?"

Kubodin frowned. "I've never thought of that before. The stone has just always been here, but in my travels over the land I've seen many buildings that were destroyed and the names of many places changed that had a connection to the emperor. They *do* destroy these things, but the folklore of the people often seems to remember. The shamans haven't found a way to stop people speaking. Yet."

"They will in time," Asana muttered. "If their power continues to grow unchecked."

"No doubt," Kubodin replied. "We've been luckier in the hills than in many other places. The grip of the shamans is not quite as tight here. That might be part of why the stone was left. That, and also because the emperor only used it once whereas the hill people have used it always."

They started to move uphill, and Shar noticed that the eastern sky was beginning to turn gray and that the drizzle had ceased and the stars had started to shine once more as the cloud cover dispersed. Something that Kubodin had said triggered a memory in her, and she thought on that as they went onward.

The emperor had *used* the stone, Kubodin had said. From what Shulu had told her, he had not just conquered lands, or joined them to the empire by diplomacy. For each clan that swore loyalty to him, he had in turn sworn loyalty back to them. He had pledged to uphold their rights and to aid them if they were attacked. He was joined to them as much as they were joined to him.

The hill steepened, and the grass was wet with rain. Shar's boots were sodden, and she would be glad when the sun rose and started to dry things out. She hoped for a little bit of sleep though before the new day began, and before Kubodin's followers started to show up. However many of them there would be.

They came to the crest of the hill. It was not large, and Shar could not see much in the night. Even so, she smiled a little to herself. This was a defensible place. It held the advantage of height on all sides. It offered visibility, at least during the day. And it was a part of the landscape held in veneration by the populace.

Not only had Kubodin seized the high ground in a military sense but also in a moral one. He had associated himself in the minds of the people with the stone, and any who came here to join his force would do so under the auspices of its traditions. Any who came to attack would feel as though they were assaulting the stone itself, and all it stood for.

Of the stone itself, they could see little except the outline of it. It was four faced though, and so far as Shar could see those faces had been cut well and evenly. It stood man high, or somewhat shorter, and though it had stood here for years beyond count, it was almost straight. It leaned to one side, but only a little.

They set up camp close to it, and there they slept. They kept turns at a watch, for their danger grew by the moment if the forces of Kubodin's brother learned of them sooner than they hoped. Yet still, they rested well, and through the remainder of the dark there was no indication of trouble.

Dawn came, and the sky was clear except for a ragged trail of clouds to the west. That was all that was left of last night's rain. The travelers, however, slept a little beyond first light. The night had been long, and today might well see battle. If not, it would see an undignified flight and the end of Kubodin's quest.

But they did not sleep long into the day. In the distance roosters crowed, and above the village the smoke of many hearth fires baking bread for the day filled the air.

Shar was curious about the stone, and went over to look at it. The smooth surface was still wet with last night's rain. There were strange symbols carved into it, but of these she could make no sense.

Kubodin joined her. "No one knows what it says, but we believe it to be written in the language of our ancestors before the Shadowed Wars."

Shar was not convinced. It looked to her something like the script she had seen on the parchment the Ahat had carried who had tried to assassinate her. The old tongue, her grandmother had called it. The tongue used by the shamans. Yet still, there was nothing to say that the people of those times had not spoken a language that the shamans had used and kept alive after the people themselves had ceased to speak it.

"How many do you think will come," Asana asked, walking up to them and changing the subject. He did not seem interested in the Oath Stone, or maybe, being the best traveled of them all, he had seen such things before.

Kubodin shrugged. "When the wind blows at the dying of the year, leaves fall. How many leaves and how strong the wind, none can say till afterward."

It was the best answer they would get until people themselves arrived. Yet that did not take long. Soon after the sun had risen properly a column of people snaked their way from the village below and began the ascent toward the Oath Stone.

Kubodin seemed indifferent, but Shar watched him closely and saw him study the column when he did not think anyone was looking at him. His fate depended on what would happen soon, and she was pleased to see that the column kept growing.

Nor was it the only one. Namarlin, or those he had deputized, had traveled through the night and sent word to other villages. Soon, there were multiple columns approaching the hill from many directions.

Asana voiced her own concern though. "So far so good. But has the enemy learned what's going on yet, and what are *they* doing about it?"

16. A Difficult Choice

Kubodin approached her, and Shar knew what he would say.

"Will you disguise yourself, as you have done before? Or will you reveal your true identity?"

She had been thinking hard on this. Without revealing herself, she could never spread word and gather an army. But the moment she *did* reveal herself, word would get back to the shamans and they would come in force against her. Here, in the Wahlum Hills, she would have time to prepare. But not much.

Also, Kubodin would benefit from this. If she sensed the mood of these hill people rightly, most of them would be keen to throw off the yoke of the shamans. And Kubodin, by associating with her, would gain an aura of mystique. *He* had brought her here. *He* was a part of the ancient prophecy that spoke of her. *She* was on his side. It would help him gather people to his banner, and make them feel as though they were fighting for a higher purpose. Yet when the battle was done, if he were the victor, might he not then cast her aside and make peace with the shamans?

"I will show myself," she replied. And silently she hoped he would not betray her.

Throughout the morning the supporters of Kubodin came, and they came in large numbers. There were columns from all the villages in the valley, and some from even beyond where the word had spread.

Kubodin greeted each group personally, and often spoke with warrior after warrior, thanking them all for coming and sharing jokes with them. Many, he seemed to know well. That was no surprise, but how friendly they were to him was another matter. He had not been here for at least a few years, but it was as though he had never left.

After they were done with him, they came to look at her. Her violet eyes shocked them, and their gazes lingered on her two swords. They were friendly to her, though awed, and many bowed.

"I'm not the-emperor-to-be in this time and place," she told them. "I'm just a warrior, fighting for justice, as you are."

She went over to speak to Kubodin when there was a quiet moment between arrivals.

"Your brother must know what's happening by now. He'll have sent some spies into the column to masquerade as your supporters and to report back to him."

"No doubt."

"You should set up a perimeter of sentries. Not to keep people out but to ensure no one leaves."

The little man considered that. "A good idea. I know many of these men, and there are many here I trust that have vouched for the others. I don't think my brother will have gotten too many spies in with them, but probably there are some."

He called a few men over. They were his age or older, and Namarlin was one of them.

"Set up a perimeter of sentries he instructed. The most trusted men you know. Let no one out of the camp, and bring any who try to leave to me."

They did as asked, and they did not question why. These men were all warriors, and they understood the purpose of the order.

"There's also the possibility of saboteurs," Kubodin said.

Shar looked around at the milling warriors. It was hard to picture any of them as agents of the enemy, but undoubtedly there would be some.

"You're right, but there's not much they can do. All that's open to them is turning sides in the midst of the battle, but that would be risky for them."

"Ha!" Kubodin laughed. "Risky all right. If they did that they'd soon be killed by those around them. And they'd also be just as likely as any of the rest to be killed by my brother's forces."

There was a great deal of activity on the top of the hill, and despite the seeming likelihood of battle the warriors sang and laughed, or else sat down on the ground and rested.

"How many warriors are here?" Nerchak asked.

"I've been keeping count as they arrived," Kubodin answered. "There are close on a thousand men here, and more coming."

At that point a tall and thickset man, at least for the Wahlum Hills from what Shar had seen, approached.

"Nomochek!" Kubodin greeted him. "It's been a long time."

The stocky man grinned broadly. "It has. Too long. But all will be well now." He looked at Kubodin's axe. "I see you still carry that tree feller."

"I do. It's felled more than trees in its time."

"So it has. I know that better than most. I've seen it, and you, in some tough situations. This will be no different, but we'll come out the other side."

"How's your wife?" Kubodin asked.

Nomochek grinned. "Just as feisty as ever. I love her, but she does have a sharp tongue if I drink too much!"

"And what else has been happening?"

"Plenty. We can catch up on that afterward. In the meantime, you should know this though. Your brother knows you're here and what you're doing. The nazram are starting to go around from hut to hut to try to intimidate people from joining you."

"Is it working?" Kubodin asked.

"Not well. So far as I can tell most people who were going to join you had already left by the time they started. You've stolen a march on him, but he's gathering his own force in Nagadar Village. He'll come against you."

"I'm counting on it," Kubodin answered. "How large is his force?"

The stocky man shrugged. "I saw them in the distance as I traveled here. It's hard to say, but I'd reckon it as large as yours."

His old friend wandered off soon after that, and Kubodin looked thoughtful.

"Are you thinking of attacking?" Asana asked him.

The little man raised his eyebrows. "Sometimes I think you can read my mind."

"Not at all. It's merely a logical tactic to consider."

Even as they spoke another group of warriors was arriving. "I think I'll ask them what they saw of the enemy forces."

Shar waited. The morning was wearing on, and she knew her friend would soon make a decision. He had been gathering information all the time from every group that came in, and by all accounts the two forces seemed about equal. This new group would likely tell the same story, and if so Kubodin would have a difficult choice to make. All the more so because whatever information he got about the enemy was hours old.

After a little while, he returned. "They say the same thing. Both forces are equal, and both continue to grow. So, what do you advise?"

Shar answered first. "Attack. Do it while you still have surprise working for you. Here, you have a defensible position. It was a great place to start in case your brother came against you quickly. But that didn't happen. The longer you wait the more the weakness of this tactic will come to the fore."

Nerchak frowned. "What weakness is that?"

"Food," Shar answered. "There's an army here, but the strongest army fails after a day or two without food. All the enemy need do is lay siege to the hill and cut off any supplies reaching us. Then we'll either starve in our great defensive position, or be forced to leave it to attack and try to break the siege."

Kubodin glanced at Asana. "What do you say, old friend?"

"I'd hate to leave here. There's so much advantage to this place, but Shar is certainly right. You need maneuverability now. There are other places you can hold and defend. You can force a battle in a place favorable to you, or you can avoid contact with your brother's forces. All the while you'll have access to resources from the valley. But here, unless your brother is overconfident or stupid enough to attack you on a hill, he'll wait you out, and starve you out."

Kubodin turned to Nerchak. "And you? What do you think?"

The young man did not look happy. Nor should he, Shar supposed. He had come with Shar to help her. He had not realized that might mean fighting for Kubodin in a battle that had nothing to do with him.

"I still think you should stay here. It's too good a position to give up. And there are supplies coming in with some of these men. If your brother besieges you here, you can last days. If he doesn't attack uphill, there are ways to try to provoke him into doing so."

Shar did not agree, and for once Nerchak had showed his inexperience. Whatever Kubodin decided though, she would support him. He had helped her when she needed it, and she would do the same for him.

The little man went over to the Oath Stone, and he leaned against it while he thought. Shar looked out over the gathering army. There was about a thousand warriors here. It seemed the enemy had a similar number, and it was surprising to her that the valley could field so many soldiers.

Kubodin returned soon after. His face was a mask, and Shar could read little in his expression except determination. He borrowed a horn from a man nearby and blew it.

Silence fell, and into it Kubodin cried out. "We go to battle! Prepare to march, and let our swift wrath fall unexpectedly upon the traitor!" Even as he spoke he brandished his axe, and the two blades gleamed wickedly in the morning sun.

"To battle! To battle!" came a thundering reply from a thousand throats, and Shar felt her own blood stir. It was one thing to discuss battles with Shulu, but it was another to be in one. This, if she survived, would be a learning experience for her. If she were to make good her ambition to destroy the shamans, she would have to fight a war.

Kubodin sorted the soldiers into a square, putting those he trusted most and knew to be the best fighters at the front. Then they marched down the hill, singing war songs with the men and walking in the first rank.

They went down the hill and came to flat land again. Then they turned and marched westward. The village the travelers had been to last night was on their left, and the encircling ridge of the valley was to their right.

Shar did not look back at the hill. No one did. So she did not see a form like a shadow cross the ground at the crest and leap nimbly atop the Oath Stone.

From that vantage, a black fox watched them, its malicious eyes sharp and intent.

17. Parley

They passed through the valley at a swift pace. Kubodin was trying his best to take the enemy by surprise. A river lay to their left now, which the men said was called the Nurthuril, and though it was not wide it provided good protection on that flank.

They rested at noon in a forest. Kubodin had ensured it was safe first by the use of scouts, and he sent them ranging out through the valley as well, especially toward the village where his brother was gathering his own army.

A flow of men still joined them, and Kubodin tried to greet each group personally as he had done earlier, but he was also busy in giving orders and hearing the reports of scouts.

Even as they prepared to leave camp and march again, word came of a large column ahead. It was feared that the enemy had marched upon them unexpectedly as Kubodin was trying to do, but it soon became apparent that this was a friendly force coming down from a village outside the valley.

"Hail, Kubodin!" their leader said when they approached. "I've been waiting for you to return for a long time."

"Hail, Tsogodin!" Kubodin replied. "I've been hoping to see you!"

So far as Shar could see they were old friends, and the newcomer's force, which was several hundred strong, joined ranks with Kubodin's army and the march began again. But those two talked earnestly as they strode ahead.

Shar estimated the army to be one and a half thousand strong now, and they looked good warriors to her. Just as back in the fens these people were poor, and their armor and weaponry were of low quality. But also, like her own people, that did not mean they were bad warriors. She looked around at them, and despite their light-hearted attitude going forward into battle, probably even today, they seemed fierce and strong to her. There was a mood to them of something finally happening that was long looked for, and they intended to make the most of it.

What the enemy was doing, and how large their force was, remained sketchy though.

Yet scouts returned soon after. They brought word the opposing army was still at their assembly point, but it was larger than expected. Estimates varied, but most put it at two thousand strong.

Kubodin did not hesitate. He hastened the pace of their march, and though no doubt enemy scouts had discovered them by now, their arrival had still been unanticipated. His brother had been more cautious and waited for greater numbers before marching. But now, he was caught with the river to his back, and according to the scouts, on lower ground than the route by which Kubodin would approach.

It did not take long to get there. Shar studied the enemy force, spread out before the river. To the left was a village, and to the right a forest. Between the two armies was open ground, and as the scouts had reported there was a gentle slope to the water.

It was not much of an advantage, but it was some. So too that the enemy did appear to have been caught by surprise. They were only now moving into a square, and Shar considered the enemy commander incompetent. Even if he had not known of Kubodin's approach, he should have guessed at the possibility and taken better steps. It was not a good place to assemble an army, and wherever they chose to assemble it should have been done in a more organized manner that had them ready to fight. Kubodin had not done so, but he had the advantage of being on a hill where no surprise could be levered against him.

None of it might make much difference though. Shar felt uneasiness churn in her stomach, for the enemy did outnumber them, and by no small amount.

She drew close to Kubodin. "We should attack swiftly," she urged.

He sighed and shook his head. "You're right, but these are my countrymen, in both armies. I don't want to spill blood, and I must try to parley first and give them the chance to surrender."

Shar understood that, but it would cost Kubodin in the end. The enemy force was larger, and it would not capitulate.

"Every minute lets them prepare better."

"I know, but the surprise was always going to be one of catching them mentally unprepared rather than physically unprepared. Even if we charged now, their square will be fully formed before we get there."

That was true, but Shar still did not like it. She did not press the point though. If this were her own people in Tsarin Fen, she might take the same risk in order to try to prevent bloodshed.

"Come with me," Kubodin asked gesturing to her. He called several others to him as well, Asana, Namarlin and Tsogodin among them.

He hastened out into the field between the two armies, and Tsogodin waved a cloth above his head. It was a signal to parley, and a promise that no attack would commence while they talked.

Out of the enemy army a group emerged to meet them. It was of a similar size, and they too waved a cloth. It was a pointless gesture because they were in no position to attack just yet. Even so, it was better to be safe than sorry.

Shar picked out Kubodin's brother straight away. He looked very much like her friend, only he wore a beard and was far better dressed. At his side was an axe too, and it must have irked him that it was a counterfeit and Kubodin had the real one.

Kubodin and Kuthondrin eyed each other darkly, and both, whether deliberately or unconsciously, gripped hard the hafts of their axes. But they did not speak.

Shar turned her gaze to the shaman. She knew it was him by the trinkets he wore. Many of his order wore items intended to awe the superstitious, and he was no different. His necklace was of bones, maybe even teeth. She could not see clearly. Moreover, she shifted her gaze to his eyes and held it there, waiting.

After a few moments of studying Kubodin, his gaze flickered disdainfully over the rest. Then they came back to her and she saw him look hard at her two swords. Then his gaze lifted and he looked direct into her eyes. Even as he did so, she smiled at him.

There was shock on his face, and Shar enjoyed it. She might die today, but to surprise a powerful enemy and see the shadow of fear fall upon him was a victory that warmed her heart.

Her smile broadened, and she saw his face redden and anger flash in his eyes. He knew his fear had been seen, and he hated her for it.

Kuthondrin broke the silence. "Surrender to me brother, and face the justice you have long put off. I don't like to see bloodshed within the clan, so I promise you that if you admit your sin and disband your followers, you can walk freely away from here into exile. For the sake of the clan, I'm willing to make that sacrifice."

Kubodin, for one of the very rare times Shar had ever seen, looked serious.

"You killed our father, and the gods will judge you for it. The clan already has, and you must know that most people have now learned the truth. You hold power only by the will of Drasta, and by the strength of the council that is corrupt. So, for the same blood of our countrymen that I would not see shed, I offer you the same choice. Disband your army and leave in exile."

"Never," Kuthondrin replied. "Yet maybe we can find some middle ground. Let us talk for a while, and explore that possibility."

Shar knew he had no intention of doing anything other than killing Kubodin, either in battle or by assassination if he left the valley to go into exile. What he wanted was to delay the battle in order to give his soldiers time to come to grips with the fact that the enemy had caught them unready.

Kubodin knew that. The love of his clan had led him into a tactical error in not attacking instantly, but he was not going to compound that error.

"If you change your mind before battle begins, have your army lay down its weapons and retreat from them. In the meantime, ponder this. Fate is on my side today. Look at my companions, and you will see."

Kuthondrin was about to reply, but before he said anything he looked into Shar's eyes and understood. Surprise lit his face, and doubt fell over him like a shadow.

He said nothing then, but simply turned and walked back toward his army. Drasta did likewise, but the retainers stared at her, dumbfounded.

"It's not too late to change side, boys," Shar said.

Drasta swung back and called them to him, and Kubodin backed away then too. He did not trust his brother to honor the conventions of parley.

Shar and the others backed away with him, and then after a little distance turned to face their own army and walked toward it. She did so with a growing sense of doubt. Once more Kubodin had used her identity to serve his own purposes, and though she could not fault him for that, she could not help but wonder if his attitude to her would change after the battle. If he won, then she would discover if she were a tool he used to regain his chieftainship just as he used the slope of the land or the element of surprise in battle.

They were only halfway back when something unexpected happened. A group of warriors broke away from the flank of Kubodin's army and charged toward them. They were some twenty strong, and as they raced headlong toward them, drawing their weapons, Shar knew Kubodin had been betrayed.

The little man knew it too. "Nazram!" he cried. "They have followed us from the coast!"

Shar drew her swords. How the nazram had found them, she could not guess. But she knew Kubodin would not have allowed them to join the ranks of his army, so they had likely slipped up from behind when they had gone out to the parley.

The army were caught by surprise, and did not act straightaway. Too late a number of them surged forward to defend Kubodin, but the nazram had a lead and they outnumbered the small group Kubodin had taken to the parley. It would be a slaughter.

And yet that small group was made up of tremendous warriors whose skill was greater than any nazram. All they needed to do was survive for a brief period, and then the nazram would have to flee into the army of Kuthondrin for protection.

Shar crouched into a fighting stance, light and poised. Yet even as she did so some instinct warned her of danger from behind. She turned, and a chill ran through her.

18. The Emperor Returns!

The shaman Drasta was without morals, but not without skill in sorcery.

Against the convention of parley he had taken advantage of the attack by the nazram to instigate his own. His head was thrown back as though in great anguish or pain, and from his hands fire dripped. The flame was crimson, twined about with black tendrils dark as any swamp bottom in the fens that had never seen the light of day.

Drasta, seemingly having summoned as much power as he could hold, lunged forward now as though throwing spears and the fire streaked through the air, sizzling as it came.

It came straight for Shar, and no matter what was happening with the nazram she knew she had to face it. As always, she placed her trust in Shulu who had taught her, and now, by extension, in the swords she had forged in antiquity.

She raised the blades crosswise before her, and gritted her teeth in fear and hope as the sorcerous flame smashed into them. The force of the blow was monstrous, and she staggered backward and almost fell. All the while the very air seemed to thrum, and a moment later a slow roll of thunder boomed over the field.

The magic in her own blades was alive. That she had always known, but it flared now in response like a hidden shield that protected her, and the dark magic soared. It wrapped around Drasta's, and became one with it.

The swords grew heavy as though made of lead, and Shar could barely hold them up. The tips lowered, and like rain flowing off a roof the magic dropped off them onto the ground. There it tore into the earth, ripping up the sod and flinging it away.

Shar fell as the earth heaved, but she rolled to her feet again instantly. Before her was a pit in the ground that might have served as her grave if not for the swords, and smoke rose from it and still the green grass around it burned in patches.

There was a cry behind her, and the sound of steel on steel. The nazram were among them, but already she counted two dead by Asana's sword, and his blade wove a death of steel more sure than Drasta's great sorcery.

Shar knew they could not survive this, attacked from behind and the front at the same time, and outnumbered. Yet a plan came to her, and a chance to live no matter how desperate it seemed.

She swung around to Drasta again, and once more crimson fire dripped from his fingers.

"Die!" he screamed, and he flung it at her in a fiery arc that ripped through the air.

She lifted her blades high and crossed them. Once more she was borne backward by the impact, but she turned and kept the swords upright. Before her, trying to flank her friends were a group of nazram. One of them was running at her, his blade held high for an overhead strike.

Shar lowered both her swords. The magic of the shaman ran the length of the blades and leaped out like a bolt of lightning. It flashed and sizzled, but this time it did not go into the ground.

It smashed into the warrior, sending him tumbling away while his hair and clothes erupted in flames. He screamed in agony, but that was cut short as he fell back among his own comrades.

He writhed on the ground, and the fire caught at some of his companions. In their surprise, Nerchak was upon them. His sword flashed and stabbed with great speed, and several fell dead before they even realized those they had thought to be easy prey were killing them.

They retreated, but then Kubodin was upon them, his axe whirring and a head of a nazram warrior flying through the air.

Shar spun around again. Her friends were much safer now. The enemy was in disarray, and within moments help would arrive. But she fixed her gaze on Drasta, fearful of yet another attack.

She need not have worried. The shaman, Kuthondrin, and their retinue were hastening back to their army. Spinning around again she saw that more nazram had died, and the rest were trying to circle around Nerchak and Kubodin. Asana was holding his own against two more where he fought, but help had finally arrived and those men were about to die.

One escaped from Nerchak, and he started to run toward the enemy army. He was too far away for Shar to engage him in a fight, yet she flipped the sword from her right hand into her left and in one smooth motion drew a knife and flung it.

The small blade spun through the air, and without the man even seeing it coming it buried itself in his neck. He reeled to the side and staggered. That was all the time Shar needed. She rushed toward him, her swords in both hands again and he died with one slicing across his neck and the other stabbing deep into his stomach.

Shar looked back at her friends. They all seemed well, but then she noticed one of the warriors Kubodin had brought with him lay still on the grass, blood staining it from a wound she could not see.

Against all odds, the nazram were dead and only one of Kubodin's warriors was. The little man cleaned his axe on the tunic of an enemy, slid the haft through the loop in his belt for it, and picked up the first of his own warriors to die and cradled him in his arms as he started to walk to his army.

Shar glanced back at Drasta. He was still hastening toward the protection of his own ranks, and Kuthondrin scurried with him. Soon the battle would begin in earnest, and far more warriors were yet to fall.

She retrieved her knife from the man she had slain, and gathered with the others to follow Kubodin. Nerchak was beside her, his hood still up and shadowing his face as it had been through the parley, and she looked at him thoughtfully.

"You said way back at Chatchek Fortress that you were a good swordsman. You didn't lie. In fact, you're a swordmaster of rare skill."

The young man merely shrugged away her compliment and did not answer.

As they walked back, the two armies were getting ready, for battle would soon break out. Yet there was a silence over the field in which they prepared, and from Kubodin's force a chant began to rise.

The emperor returns! The emperor returns!

They had seen Shar's eyes, and they had seen the twin swords. That had been enough to convince them, yet now they had seen something more. The magic of the Swords of Dawn and Dusk had been invoked before them, and they had seen the shaman thwarted in his purpose. They *believed* now. They remembered the prophecy of old, and they knew what it would mean if it were fulfilled. They knew what it would mean for them and the shamans, and they liked it.

The booming of their chant grew loud until it rolled out more ominously than the thunder of Drasta's sorcery, and the enemy army heard it. Those who had been with Drasta and Kuthondrin would speak of her eyes, and the army would wonder if destiny was against them today. That would sap their confidence despite their greater numbers, and Kubodin's plan, if plan it was, could not have gone better for him.

19. Battle and Blood

The two armies faced each other. Above, the ravens began to circle.

Shar felt that great cold settle over her that always came at times of peril. Her emotions were submerged, and logic and the warrior spirit came to the ascendancy. Some soldiers trained all their careers to try to attain this state. Stillness in the Storm some called it. But for her, it was a feeling that she had felt since childhood.

She stood at the front of the square with Kubodin to her right. On the little man's right was Asana. Beyond him was Nerchak. All around were some of the finest and most battle-tested warriors in the clan.

Kubodin slowly raised his axe. "We fight for justice!" he cried.

We fight for justice! came the booming answer of the army.

"We fight for the freedom of our people from shaman enslavement," Kubodin called out.

Over the field an answer rolled deeply. *We fight for the freedom of our people from shaman enslavement.*

"And we fight with the emperor and destiny on our side!"

And we fight with the emperor and destiny on our side! came the vast echo.

Shar heard it, and even in her detached state she felt the awe of it. Yet, so too, that niggle of doubt was there. Was Kubodin using her? If she lived, she would find out. But right now she merely observed these thoughts as though they belonged to another. All that really mattered just now were the swords in her hands and the litheness of her body that was ready for the demands soon to be placed upon it.

Kubodin shook his axe. "Advance!" he ordered.

And the army advanced.

They did not run. The hill tribes used bows and arrows for hunting, but they did not favor that weapon in battle. So there was no rush to beat a hailstorm of arrows. Nor would spears be thrown. It would be a simple clash of brute force, of warrior against warrior in the embrace of battle.

Shar marched forward in unison with the others, holding the front rank of the square in perfect line with the rest. Her detachment was so great that she saw the enemy begin to advance also, Kuthondrin in the front ranks opposite, holding high his axe just like Kubodin. Death was coming toward her, but she was light of heart.

Even so, that part of her mind that coldly calculated noted that Kuthondrin had not set himself in the exact middle as Kubodin had, and the two enemies would not face each other. Likewise, she made plans to change the way the hill men fought. If ever they came to fight beneath her banner, she must train them to the uses of, and the defenses against, bowmen and spear throwers.

The two forces drew close, and Shar could see into the eyes of the opponents. This, however, she avoided. She looked only at their chests. To gaze into the eyes of the enemy was a mistake, for it could allow them the opportunity to dominate by instilling fear. Also, the chest was a center point from which any attack by arm or leg could equally be seen the moment it was instigated.

Many of the warriors on either side had shields, and against these they hammered the flats of their swords to create a chaotic din. It was meant to intimidate the enemy, and to bring a surge of blood flowing into the arm muscles of the warrior. Shar did not have a shield though. Instead, she flipped the blade in her left hand up against the forearm. In this position it would serve as a kind of shield. Nor was there any room for her to use two swords to attack anyway without endangering those to her side.

The two forces came together in a scream of blades and shouts that tore the air. Shar stabbed at the chest of the man opposite, and he used his shield to deflect it. A moment later he stabbed at her, thinking her an easy kill because she lacked a shield, but this she deflected easily with her left arm, and with her right sword she stabbed low, cutting the man's thigh. He stepped back, but even as he did so the tip of her blade flicked up again, taking him in the groin. He screamed, lowering his shield even more, and her sword circled up and ripped out his throat in a spray of blood.

All around her blood was flowing. The stench of entrails was in the air, and she saw one man in the enemy ranks with his guts spilling out and tripping over them as a sword cracked into his head ending the pain and horror he must have felt.

Shar was deep in Stillness in the Storm, and she floated above the horrors that she saw. She merely fought, keeping herself relaxed and flowing with the battle. When it was necessary, she parried. When there was an opening, she struck. She did not count the men that died before her, nor did she do more than notice when men fell in her own line and were replaced by a fresh warrior from the row behind.

There was only the battle. There was only the play of swords. Shar did not heed the screams of anguish, the stink of entrails or soiled trousers. She did not see the circling of the ravens above or hear the cry of the red kites that were also battlefield scavengers. She merely breathed, fought and killed.

Yet she did hear the blowing of a horn that signaled it was time for the front row to fall back and let the next row come forward.

She slipped back and a new warrior took her place. She glanced to her right and saw Kubodin, his face covered in blood but none of it his own. He was a man who loved to fight, but he was quiet and grim now.

He did not go back through the ranks but stayed close so he could direct the fight. Asana was there also, his face betraying nothing of what he felt. Nerchak had survived also, and he looked nearly as calm as Asana. Again Shar marveled at the poise of one so young, and wondered where he had learned to fight so well.

Shar turned her gaze to the battle. The dead were many, and the living fought with fury to try to keep themselves that way. No one had the advantage yet, and though the battle line had moved back and forth a little, it was barely more than a few paces each way. She could not say who would win at this point, but she waited.

If Drasta attacked with sorcery, things would turn fast. But it was forbidden to do so. She did not trust him though, and she thought that if he were desperate enough he might go against tradition. Yet since the fall of the emperor a thousand years ago, sorcery against soldiers on the field of battle was outlawed. No clan, however much oppressed by a shaman, would stand for that.

The battle ebbed and flowed. Still she waited, as did Kubodin. There was always a time when opportunity, if it were recognized, might be seized. It could not be forced, but when that turning point arose it must be seen and taken instantly. Likely, it would not come again.

Shar saw it when it came, but Kubodin and Asana had seen it an instant earlier. A huge man, at least for these hills, broke rank with his fellows and he laid about him with a war hammer. It was an unusual weapon, but he had the size and strength to wield it with great skill. He disdained the use of a shield, and his armor was of hardened leather. It withstood the sword thrusts intended to kill him. But few were aimed at him, for to get close enough to do so meant that the hammer would fall upon them, and even if the man were killed that hammer would still fall and slay them in turn.

Men died beneath the war hammer, their skulls crushed and their chests shattered. The warrior came forward, and Kubodin's men, seeking to avoid him, backed away. The line buckled, and the enemy, sensing possible victory, surged forward.

It was a time of flux, and all might be lost. Yet Kubodin knew it was an opportunity also. At least Shar thought so, for she understood what he was doing.

The little man slipped into the front row again, and he charged at the enemy warrior. The war hammer came down, and it slid past Kubodin's head and brushed his shoulder, but the axe was in motion, and it hewed at the enemy's leg, severing it below the knee. Yet before the warrior could fall the reverse stroke of the axe came back and smashed through the armor to sink deep into his chest.

The warrior fell, and the war hammer dropped to the ground.

"Your chief is victorious!" cried Shar, and she slew an enemy before her.

The warriors about her rallied seeing Kubodin beat such a great enemy, and at the same moment the heart went out of the opposition. Just when victory was in their grasp they had received a setback.

Kubodin had never had all of Shar's expert training from a mind that had lived more than a thousand years, yet still he knew exactly what to do. This was the moment.

"Advance!" Kubodin ordered.

All around him his warriors strode forth, filling the void that had surrounded the giant enemy. Horns blew to carry the message up and down the line, and the army surged forward.

The surge did not last long. The enemy resisted it, and the fighting was bloody and brutal. Yet resist as they might, they had not stopped it completely.

Inch by inch Kubodin's army pressed forward, and he was at the center of it fighting fiercer than the rest. Once more Shar, Asana and Nerchak were with him, and they fought so hard that they were at risk of penetrating deep into the enemy ranks and then being surrounded and killed.

They slowed down, and the line caught up with them. The warriors who supported Kubodin could sense victory swing their way now, and they fought harder. If they could advance an inch, they knew they could advance a foot. And if that, a stride.

So it went, and as the minutes passed by that seemed as hours, the enemy began to retreat. It was slow at first, and Kuthondrin did well to hold them together, yet at the last nothing could be done and the square began to lose shape as those at its rear retreated faster than those at the searing front of the fighting, harangued by their leader to hold fast and fearful to turn their backs.

Panic set in. And then it became a route, Kuthondrin running with them and cursing as he went. The enemy fled. The village to their left and the river at the back hemmed them in, so they headed right, and entered the forest.

Kubodin harried them as best he could, but he was not so foolhardy as to pursue them into the cover of the trees. It was possible that an ambush was set there, but Shar doubted that very much.

The army came to a halt and cheered. Shar felt no elation though, for the sense of Stillness in the Storm fell away from her. She looked around now at the battlefield, and the horror of it struck her as a blow.

The dead were everywhere. The injured were, perhaps, more horrific. There were men whose arms had been hacked off. Others convulsed on the ground, or writhed in agony. Some sat, rocking back and forth with no obvious injury. Their wound was to the mind, which though unseen was just as devastating. And already, at the rear where the battle had passed over them and left them behind, the dead were being swarmed over by ravens.

Kubodin acted quickly. He gave orders for the help of the wounded, but the enemy was not far from his mind either. He sent out scouts through the forest to see what they were doing.

He gathered the army together, all those who were still fit to fight. And he marched, shunning the forest and skirting around it. The quicker he went after the enemy the greater the chance he could gain a swift and complete victory and minimize further bloodshed.

There was no time to bury the dead. The ravens would feast, but the wounded were left with a guard for protection and to help dress wounds.

The scouts began to return, and they advised that the forest had been clear. Shar was glad that Kubodin had avoided it though. He had lost time, but not a lot.

Soon after, word came back of where the enemy was heading. Kubodin did not seem surprised. The Bald Hill, the scouts called it.

"What is it?" Asana asked. "Is there a fortress there?"

Kubodin shook his head. "Not a fortress. At least, not a building. It's an ancient hill fort. There are ramparts of earth and a final small plateau. It's a strong place to defend, and the nearest in reach for Kuthondrin."

Shar did not like it. It was still possible the enemy might surrender, but this did not signal it. Perhaps Kuthondrin's commanders would talk him out of continuing, and certainly there would be those who would urge it given their loss just now. But Shar knew better. Even if Kuthondrin was willing to go into exile, if Kubodin would still allow that, Drasta would not. No shaman could surrender to a force that had as one of its members the heir to the emperor.

20. The Night Walker Clan

The army pressed on, and Bald Hill soon came into view.

Shar saw immediately how it got its name. In a land where forests were common, the entire hill was pure grassland. Yet the distinctive earth ramparts, dug in ages past and covered in turf like the rest, stood out as an unusual feature.

There was no chance of overtaking the enemy before they reached the hill's safety. Likewise, the day was wearing on and one battle had already been fought. There would not be another.

Kubodin seemed to read her thoughts. "We'll lay siege here this afternoon. We can't do any more, but that'll be enough. We can isolate them and prevent any new forces bolstering their numbers during the night."

They came to the hill, and it was larger than it seemed. The defenses were primitive, being merely a series of ditches dug into the sides of the hill and the removed soil used to form a ramp immediately above the ditch. Despite that, they were highly effective. Shar knew it would be a tough fight to overcome an enemy with that advantage.

But they did not really need to. The enemy had little in the way of supplies, and hunger would soon strike at them.

"Is there a source of water up there?" Shar asked.

"There's a well, but it's deep and provides little water. It won't last them long."

Kubodin did not seem as reassured as he should be, and Shar began to have doubts as well. Why had Kuthondrin come here? Certainly it was defensible, but if he had stayed elsewhere in the valley where he could not have been surrounded he could have retained access to food, water and people. But he had not. Did he know something they did not? Were there reinforcements on the way?

The hill was too large, or rather Kuthondrin's army too few, to man the lower ramparts. He had gone to the plateau and would use just the last ditch as his defense.

Kubodin trod warily up the hill, and he gave orders for his army to encircle it. This was a dangerous period, for the enemy could try to break out and it would be difficult to get enough men quickly to whichever area they chose to try to escape through. If Kuthondrin tried that it would only show though that he had made a grave error in coming here and undermine the morale of his men even further than it had been already by their recent loss.

It was late afternoon by the time the perimeter was properly established, and the first shadows of dusk were creeping over the valley below. Kubodin had ordered a large party to fell trees in the valley and bring them up for campfires. That would serve for cooking purposes but also to light the hill so that any movement of the enemy could be seen.

Not long after sunset word from scouts came in that another army had marched toward the hill. It was the Night Walker Clan, and they would arrive by mid-morning tomorrow.

Kubodin took the news calmly, and Shar realized he had expected something of the kind. So had she, and it put the enemy's retreat to the hill fortress in a different light. They did not have to hold the position for long, and supplies were not an issue. Kubodin could not risk being caught between both forces, even if the new one was only about five hundred strong, as reports suggested.

"Who are these Night Walkers?" Asana asked.

Kubodin thought for a moment. "They're a strange tribe. Small compared to the Two Ravens, but fierce. They live to the south in a land wilder even than this. They're unpredictable, and they survive by being that way. They're under a lot of pressure by different tribes, but they always have an alliance going with one or the other. It seems they're currently on good terms with Kuthondrin."

Asana gazed out into the growing dusk. "You could try to negotiate with them. Offer them something they want, or maybe even take the risk of dividing your force and sending a small army back to counter them while you lay siege here."

"Maybe," Kubodin replied, but he did not seem convinced.

Shar did not like the idea much either. It might work, but it was a gamble.

"I have another idea," she offered.

Kubodin looked at her intently, and she realized the same plan had occurred to him.

"You could try a night attack. I know the men are weary, but once more it would surprise Kuthondrin. If it succeeded, the Night Walkers would not have any reason to fight. On the contrary, they would be more likely to try to negotiate an alliance with the new chief."

"And if it failed?" Nerchak asked.

"Then there would be time to decamp here and either attack the Night Walkers or maneuver until circumstances were more favorable."

"None of the choices are great," Kubodin said. "The hill tribes aren't fond of night battles. No one is, really. Especially after a day that's already seen fighting. But that's exactly why Kuthondrin won't expect it."

The light was failing fast and they gazed up at the earth rampart that was not so far away. It was ringed with the enemy, and it did not look easy to take. Yet still, Shar had noted that years of erosion had made the ditches shallower than they had been and the thrown up dirt had flattened.

"We need a closer look while there's still some daylight," Kubodin said.

Once more a small parley group was gathered, and a cloth waved to signal it. They climbed up the rest of the hill, pausing for a little while until the enemy waved a cloth to signal that the parley was accepted.

Shar did not trust the enemy. Drasta had broken the peace during the last one, and he would be doubly inclined to do so now. His own warriors would despise him if he did though, and already his previous actions would have cost him. Discontent in the enemy ranks would be festering, and for a number of reasons. At any rate, if Drasta attacked she could defend herself. And perhaps Kubodin could also. Shulu had made his axe just as she had made the Swords of Dawn and Dusk.

She studied the defenses as best she could. The ditch and rampart were worn away in places by the rush of water down the hill in times of heavy rain. Mostly, it was still serviceable, but in those places where erosion had damaged it the enemy had contrived additional barricades of timber planks. Evidently there had been some sort of a building up on the plateau, but it had been pulled down to shore up the weak spots in the earth works.

They soon came near the rampart, and the enemy leered down at them. Nearby, erosion had done its work and Shar studied the timber barricade placed there closely, but then her attention shifted as Kuthondrin appeared and spoke.

"Well, dog," he said, "let's see how good you are at digging. We're secure here."

Kubodin retained his calm. "You are secure, brother, but without much food and water."

"Is that so? Perhaps things have changed in the years since last you were here."

Shar noticed that neither side referenced the approaching Night Walkers. Kuthondrin would hope that they had not been discovered, and Kubodin would hope that his brother could not be sure they were coming.

"There has been much suffering," Kubodin said, changing the subject. "Good warriors lie dead and dying. There's no need for more of that. Let just the two of us fight, warrior to warrior, axe to axe, and allow the gods to decide who is the victor and who will sit in the chief's chair of the Two Ravens Clan."

The sun had sunk below the horizon now, and the shapes of the men on the rampart above were ill lit despite the many fires on both the slopes and on top of the plateau. Shar could not see Kuthondrin clearly, but she sensed the sneer on his face as he answered.

"Not likely, little brother. Rest well and see what the morrow brings," then he swung away and left them. His men on the rampart jeered and offered a few insults, but Kubodin merely shrugged and backed away. There was no sign of Drasta, but caution was always well advised. On seeing that, some of the men jeered even more loudly, yet Shar noticed that many were quiet.

Drasta had made an error, and a lot of the soldiers had not liked his earlier attack. These men were warriors, and they respected men who fought and died by their courage and the skill of their arms. Sorcery took away from that, and they likely thought it cowardly. At least it would be thought so back in Tsarin Fen, and Shar did not think it was any different here.

They made their way back to the camp, and Kubodin seemed deep in thought.

"Are you going to commit to the night attack?" she asked.

"I am. I don't think he'll be expecting it, and he's putting all his hope in the Night Walkers tomorrow."

"Good," Shar said. "Because I have a plan to offer you."

21. A Swift Knife

It was dark now, and had been for some good while. All seemed peaceful and quiet, but word had gone around Kubodin's army of what he wanted.

There was reluctance, just as he had expected, to the idea of a night attack. Yet he had ensured that news of the Night Walkers had gone around with the order to prepare for battle. And also the idea that good men had died today at the enemy's hands, and that if they were to be avenged it must be tonight. Battle could not be risked tomorrow with another force on the way.

Once used to the idea, Shar sensed that the men were now keen. It was better to get this over and done with than to endure a night of fitful sleep where the fears of battle would haunt their dreams.

When all was ready, Kubodin had one of his trusted men blow the horn that signaled the attack. More wood was thrown on the fires to provide greater light, and the men who had been lingering in the deeper shadows between the fires rushed forward.

The advance was swift and loud, with a great deal of shouting and the clashing of sword on shield. Yet the enemy had set a proper defense, and though taken unawares they were ready.

Battle broke out all along the top rampart circling the hill. Screams filled the night, and men died by the flickering light of the fires that now blazed with the extra fuel added to them.

The enemy had a great advantage. But Kubodin's men fought bravely. Almost, it seemed that they would break through the defenses in places, but always they were beaten back.

Shar expected that to happen, and Kubodin waited with her, not taking part in the fight. Around them were their friends, and a hundred of the fiercest warriors in Kubodin's army. They were tense as a drawn bow, but the plan Shar had devised was not quite ready to be loosed yet.

Then the horns came, first to the left and a moment later to the right. In these places the last of the reserves had been released, and they rushed into the battle.

Kubodin watched, his dark eyes glinting and his axe in his hand.

"They are nearly through in those two places!" he said.

So it was, but Kuthondrin drew on reserves and bolstered those areas. Soon, any chance of a breakthrough seemed less likely.

This was the moment Shar had planned for though. The enemy's focus was on those two places, and their reserves had been committed. Kubodin saw it just as she did, and he gave the command to the small group around them.

"Forward!" he ordered. And he ran ahead, grabbing one of the branches that had earlier been laid into the fire to burn on one end only. The others did the same, and then the group of a hundred were racing ahead, torches in hand.

Shar ran beside him, and they headed straight for the weakest point in all the defenses, which was the area where erosion had nearly leveled the earth rampart and timber had been placed there as a barricade. A hundred burning torches were thrown over it, some hitting the front and some the top. Shar wedged her torch between two slats of timber, and brushed the wood with her fingers.

It was dry, as she had hoped. Kuthondrin should have doused the barricade with water to hinder such an attack as this, but water was in short supply at the top of the hill and it was reserved for warriors. Perhaps they would have used some in the morning to douse the timber, expecting an attack then and not wanting to use it unnecessarily before that time.

It was a mistake Shar had been hoping for, and one that Kuthondrin might yet rue. But it was too early to tell yet.

The enemy were surprised, and there was much shouting behind the barricade. They were not unprepared though, for they had some buckets or vessels filled with water and ready. These were splashed over the timber in an attempt to put the fire out.

It was touch and go. There seemed to be only so many prepared vessels, and fewer than Kuthondrin would have wished for. Yet it took time for fire to properly catch, and especially at the top of the barricade the flames were suppressed quickly. Even so, the flames at the front were difficult to reach from behind the barricade, and as men leaned over to drop their water Kubodin and his men made them risk their lives. There were few spears available, but some, and these took a deadly toll. Other warriors threw knives and rocks.

It was a strange battle, and as it swung back and forth between growing flames and splashing water Shar bided her time. She had two knives, and she made each one count. She was as close to the flames as she dared stand, and each blade flew through the flickering light to kill a man.

But the barricade was catching, and the enemy focused on that point to try to douse it. Even as they did so Kubodin gave a great cry, and axe in hand he leaped at a section of the wall that had less defenders behind it and hewed at the timber. A slat shattered at his stroke, and the makeshift post behind it was cut down swiftly too. A hole appeared in the wall, and Kubodin pressed into it, axe swinging and hewing timber no longer but men.

Kubodin surged into the enemy, and Shar came through the gap behind him. Together they faced the desperate mass of their opponents, swords leaping like streaking stars and the double-bladed axe descending like a fiery comet leaving a trail of blood in its wake.

They could not prevail for long. Yet they created a gap, and more came in behind them, including Asana and Nerchak. At the same time the fire had done damage to some of the barricade, and using swords and boots the men tore it down, and the hundred of them surged forward over ground that was near level and gave only a small advantage to the enemy.

The fighting was brutal, and warriors died swiftly. Yet Kuthondrin's men, desperate to hold, began to push back. Even as they did so a cry came up from the fight maybe a hundred paces to the left, and Shar knew that another breakthrough had occurred.

The fight went out of the enemy then, and horns were blowing across the top of the plateau. It might be that more breakthroughs had occurred farther away that Shar could not see.

A slow retreat began, and the enemy fell back into a square in the middle of the plateau, surrounded now by Kubodin's men who flowed in from all directions.

This was a dangerous moment. It was the last stand of the enemy, yet Kubodin had no control of his spread out forces. All they had were the plans set before the battle began, and if something unexpected happened it could all fall apart.

Kubodin was covered in blood and looked fiercer than Shar had ever seen him. Nerchak fought beside him now, and Shar marveled at the young man's skill with his blade. The enemy fell before him and those who lived feared to come against him.

Kuthondrin was suddenly before them now, and above the din of battle Shar heard him exhort his men. Just as suddenly Drasta was there, but Kubodin had not seen him and charged at his brother.

The shaman raised his hands and crimson fire flared, then he thrust them forward and the deadly sorcery leapt forward at Kubodin. Too late the little man sensed his danger. He was turning and raising his axe, but he would not be fast enough.

Shar was there though. She darted forward, swords raised, and came between the sorcerer and his prey. The force of the dark magic smote at her, and she had not had time to brace herself. Like a toppling mountain it crashed into her and sent her sprawling, her head smacking the ground and flames twining about her.

She struggled to her feet, vulnerable and unsure how badly she was hurt. The world spun around her, and her body ached. Dimly she saw Drasta draw himself up and summon more sorcerous fire. She was not sure she could survive another strike, but then the shaman stepped back with a look of surprise on his face.

Nerchak was there, and swift as thought a knife sped from his hand. Like a viper striking it darted at the shaman's neck, and the blade struck home in a spray of blood. That look of surprise was still on Drasta's face even as he fell and died.

Kubodin was there now too, concern on his face and his arm on her shoulder to steady her.

"I saw what you did," he said. "I'll not forget."

She shook her head. "Forget about me now. Kuthondrin is over there. It's time to finish this."

Kubodin gave her a searching look, and then he spun, his axe dripping blood, and he ran into the fray. Kuthondrin saw him, and raised high his own axe.

22. On Bended Knee

The battle was nearly done now, and its outcome decided. Kubodin had won the victory, and only because of that Kuthondrin faced him.

Even so, the fighting still continued. "Have done with this!" Kubodin cried. "Surrender, and save the lives of many. I still offer you exile."

"Never!" Kuthondrin replied, and his axe gave answer also. It arced through the air in a great stroke that was so fast for such a large weapon that it would have killed many. But Kubodin merely swayed to the side and let it pass, then thrust forward a swift jab of his own axe.

Shar did not want to watch this battle between brothers, but she could not take her eyes off it. Kuthondrin nimbly leaped back out of harm's way, and he swung the axe in slow circles before him.

There was no point to this, unless it was Kuthondrin's pride. Maybe he would rather die than face exile. Or maybe he believed that if he beat Kubodin his force would rally and hold their square until help came from the Night Walkers.

Whatever the case, the two of them fought, and never had Shar seen such a display of skill before. The axe was a deadly weapon in the hands of a warrior well trained to use it. For anyone else it was slow and clumsy. Yet these were two masters, and the cut and thrust and dance of evasion and attack played back and forth with a grace that hid the deadly intent.

Kuthondrin was larger and stronger, but Kubodin was faster and more agile. They seemed perfectly matched, but there was no such thing.

No two warriors were ever equal. Or if they were, their weapons were not. So it was here, for Kuthondrin raised his axe to block a blow that came too fast to evade. Metal struck metal, and it seemed to Shar that beside the sparks that flew there was a flash of light.

Kuthondrin's axe disintegrated, one of the blades spinning off slowly to land some distance away with the haft. But the other part flew back hard to strike Kuthondrin a mighty blow. He staggered back, the gleam of bone showing near his left temple, then blood ran in gushes from the wound.

The chief of the Two Ravens tribe fell slowly to his knees.

"May the gods forgive me," he muttered, and then fell forward.

He was dead, but heedless of the battle Kubodin laid down his axe and cradled his brother in his arms. He wept, and Shar saw the side of him that he always hid. No matter his gruffness. No matter his tendency to make a joke of everything. Deep down inside of him there was a well of emotion, and Shar wept herself for what he had endured. His father had been murdered. He had been falsely accused of the crime. And justice, when it finally came, brought the death of his brother.

Asana knelt beside his friend, and placed an arm around his shoulders.

Shar could not bear to watch anymore. She looked around at the battle instead, and saw that many of the enemy were surrendering. They had seen their shaman and their chief die. It was all over.

The fires burned low, but at length the sun rose in a red sky to the east. Kuthondrin's men had laid down their weapons and gathered together in the middle of the plateau. Kubodin, with a guard of his own men, walked among them and spoke to them at some length. The rest of the army was busy tending the wounded and disposing of the bodies of the fallen.

Much timber was being cut and several great biers were being built on which the dead would be burned. There were not enough shovels to bury them, and to let them lie was to risk the spread of disease. Nor was it fitting. These men, on both sides, were still warriors of the Two Ravens Clan.

Of the Night Walkers, there was as yet no sign. There was little worry among the men about them though. They were too few to pose a serious threat, and more than likely they would be willing to talk given that their alliance with Kuthondrin was now over.

Kubodin joined Shar after a while and asked her to come over to the warriors who had surrendered and reveal herself. They would have heard the rumors, and they had seen the magic of the swords from a distance. But they had not met her yet.

She went with her friend, but she wondered what he had in mind. Would he use her to help him unite the tribe under his leadership?

They came to where the men sat, forlorn and despondent.

"I have told you of her," Kubodin called out to them, his voice loud and carrying across the assembled warriors. "It is a triseptium year, and the Swords of Dawn and Dusk have been found. The heir of the emperor has come!"

Slowly, Shar drew her swords. The blades gleamed in the morning light, and the amethyst pommel stones caught the sun and burned with a blue fire. It was at her eyes that those closest to her looked though, and she saw the fear on their faces.

Or it might have been awe, for many of them stood up only to go down on one knee to salute her in the traditional fashion.

She saluted them back, raising the swords higher in the air.

"Hail, Two Ravens warriors! Stand up. Do not bend the knee to me, for today I am a warrior as you are, and nothing more than that. Nor less than that. Have I not fought today, risked my blood as you have? Have I not felt the clash of swords, as you have? Have I not fought for another to earn my daily bread, as you have?"

The surrendered army stirred, and many stood now to listen to her, but many remained on their knee. She looked over them all, catching many by the eye though few held her gaze.

"I am not the emperor. I am the emperor that could be, if you want me. Yesterday we were enemies. Today? Today we can be friends. Do you want me, warriors? Do you want an end to war? Do you tire of the struggles between tribes? Those struggles occur all over the lands of the empire that existed of old. And why? By dividing us, the shamans make us weak. By setting us against ourselves, they make themselves strong. Do you want to end that? Do you want *me* instead?"

She flipped her blades in the air. They spun in a circle, and she caught them and sheathed them in the same motion. Then she tossed her hair back and bowed gracefully to them.

"Yes!" came many scattered replies. "We want you!"

The chanting grew louder, and then a new voice boomed over the top of them. It was Kubodin, and he knelt before her.

"I am the chieftain of these people now, by our ancient laws. But your right to be emperor is older still. In your body flows the blood of Chen Fei. I will serve you. I pledge my life to you. The Two Ravens Clan acknowledges you, and will go into battle at your command. We are the first to do so, but we will not be the last!"

Shar was surprised. She had questioned Kubodin's motives, but now she knew that was without foundation. Before she could answer though, another chant rose from the crowd, and soon the surrendered army and the victorious army took it up as one.

Shar Fei! Shar Fei! Shar Fei!

23. Then Kill Me

There was much to do in a short space of time, and Kubodin made decisions quickly.

First, he established a field hospital close to where the well was on the top of the hill. It had gone dry due to overuse, but would likely replenish if left alone for a few hours.

The rest of the warriors would leave swiftly. Kubodin obtained a pledge from the surrendered army that the fighting was done and that they supported him. On receiving that, they were allowed to collect their weapons and join to Kubodin's force. They were one now, and no treachery was expected. It was not the nature of Two Ravens warriors to be duplicitous. However, the nazram that had formed Drasta's guard remained as prisoners. They were not trusted.

The army headed down the hillside, and they moved to a location where a stream provided water. After replenishing their supplies, Kubodin retired to a nearby slope that was clear of trees and offered a good place to defend. He did not expect a fight with the Night Walkers. They were badly outnumbered now, but all the hill tribes were fierce fighters, and it would have been incompetent to take a lesser position.

It was not long before scouts brought news of the approaching force. No doubt, their own scouts had determined that a battle had been fought and that Kubodin was the victor. What they would do though, no one could guess.

Shar studied the new force as it came into view. She could see little of it because they had ceased to march quite some distance away. A wise move, and one that signaled their chief did not wish his intentions to be misconstrued. Even so, he was not on his own lands, and had marched into another tribe's territory. Tensions were high.

The flags of parley were shown, and Kubodin went forward onto the ground between the armies with the same small group that he had done when meeting his brother, save for the single warrior who had died.

An equal sized part came forward from the Night Walkers.

"Who is the Night Walker chief?" Asana asked.

"His name is Sagadar. I've met him once before, but it was long ago. He'll be old now, but he was born cunning and the years will only have added to that."

Shar picked him out as his group approached. The rest were young warriors, and the chief was the only older man. He wore a beard, and it had turned silver. Yet still he walked briskly and with confidence.

They came together and introductions were given. Shar felt the old man's eyes on her, but he gave no start at the color of hers or her name. His scouts, or spies, had learned of her.

"You are on Two Ravens land, Sagadar," Kubodin said to begin the parley. His tone was not one of accusation. He merely stated a fact.

"I am," Sagadar replied. "I was invited here."

"No doubt. The situation has changed, however. I'm now the chief of the tribe, and your assistance is no longer required. Nevertheless, I thank you for being willing to come to the aid of the Two Ravens when they were in … difficulty."

They both knew this was not quite the truth. The Night Walkers had come here to seek advantage for themselves.

For, had Kuthondrin survived, he would now be in their debt.

"The tribes of the Wahlum Hills must be ever ready to help one another, when circumstances allow."

Kubodin nodded gravely. "So you will withdraw then, now that your assistance is no longer needed?" It was asked as a question, but by accident or design Kubodin's hand fell to the haft of his axe. His true meaning was that they had best go, and go quickly.

Sagadar inclined his head. "We will leave swiftly."

Shar had been considering what to do, and she intervened at this point. The Two Ravens Clan had joined her, but she needed more, so much more than that.

"Now that Sagadar is here, Kubodin, perhaps he and his retinue might wish to stay for a while? Maybe if you got to know each other better, you could both find ways to help your tribes?"

Kubodin was not surprised. She realized he had been expecting her to say something.

For the first time though, Sagadar looked at her closely and his gaze was not friendly.

"I know who you claim to be, so let's not be vague here. What you want is for me to acknowledge you as emperor, and I will not do that."

Shar smiled at him, but it was a hard smile. "Do you doubt who I am, even after looking into my eyes?"

"Your eyes don't prove anything. It might just be that you escaped the attention of the shamans somehow."

"That might be, but it is also a triseptium year. And I have these."

She stepped back. She did not wish this to be seen as an attack. Slowly, she withdrew her swords.

"These are the Swords of Dawn and Dusk. You may doubt my eyes, but there are no other weapons such as these. And if you doubt them, then you can soon prove their authenticity by touching them."

The chief's face hardened at that. He knew the legend that it was death for any but the heir of the emperor to lay a hand on those blades.

He was not moved though. "You might be who you claim to be. Even so, I want nothing to do with you and the war you will bring."

"Then will you not fight for your people? Will you allow the shamans to divide the nation, setting tribe against tribe? How many warriors have died in their cause over the years? Do you not see how they manipulate everyone to increase their own power, and diminish the power of the people?"

Sagadar did not like that, yet he hesitated to answer. Whatever he thought personally, he also had to anticipate what his tribe would think. It was not unheard of for chiefs to be cast down and a new one chosen.

"You say many things. Some may be true, or not. I think you are a liar and a fraud, but maybe some of my tribe will believe you."

Shar began to sense what he was doing. Word of what he said would eventually reach the ears of his shaman, so he was trying to guard himself. At the same time, he was trying not to shut the door to her completely, lest she really was who she claimed to be. If that were the case, he did not wish to face her wrath if she came to power.

But noncommittal prevarication was not an option. She would not stand for it. If she moved too slowly, her enemies would destroy her.

"We have talked long enough, Sagadar. I will not try to convince you with words. They are empty. Only actions count. For the Cheng nation, I would die. That is my destiny. But I cannot overthrow the shamans without help. So choose! Not for yourself, but for your people."

She cast aside her swords and knelt before him. "Choose! Kill me now and serve the shamans forever, or pledge your service to me and the future I would bring."

24. Judge My Character

Sagadar hesitated, and Shar waited with all the patience she could summon.

This would be nothing like when she had surrendered herself to the ghost of the general at Chatchek Fortress. There, she had been moved by a sense of fate to offer herself up to his mercy. Here, it was a calculated gamble. And one that might go wrong.

If so, she was not meekly surrendering to destiny as before. There was a technique, unarmed as she was, to deflect the tip of the sword by hollowing her chest and turning her waist. It was a tactic of last resort, but it could be done. Then she would kill him. Such a feat of daring and display of martial skill might sway whoever took his place as chief to come to her side. Maybe.

Sagadar looked grim, and she could see that he wanted to kill her. He wished no part of the changes she would bring if she came to power. But she had forced his hand. He could not walk the narrow path between appeasing her and the shamans at the same time. If he did not kill her when presented with the opportunity, the shamans would punish him. Yet if he tried, he would upset those in his tribe who hated the shamans.

She watched him coolly, and he made the mistake of looking into her gaze. She held it, and there was not a shadow of fear in her glance. That would disturb him, and their color would compound that. He knew she was the true heir to the emperor, and he knew the prophecy. If he tried to subvert it, might not destiny trample him down in turn?

The longer he hesitated, the more confident she grew. Twice, the muscles in his arm tensed and he gripped the hilt hard, but each time he thought better of striking her.

He cast down his sword onto the ground. "I am not a killer of unarmed women," he said. "No matter who they claim to be."

He still tried to walk that narrow path, but Shar would not let him. She stood and retrieved her swords.

"No," she replied. "I am no ordinary woman, though. I am Shar Fei, and I shall be emperor. The shamans have sent word to you of who I am, and ordered you to kill me if you see me. Is it not so?"

"It is so," he said quietly.

"But you did not because you felt my destiny. And I tell you this truly. Accept me now, and pledge your allegiance to me, or I will walk straight to your waiting warriors. *They* will not hesitate. They will cast you aside and bend their knees to me, for I will deliver them from the shamans and the troubles of the land." She saw the shock on his face, and knew that no one had ever dared speak to him that way before. Out of the corner of her eye she also saw Kubodin go pale. No one spoke to a chief of a fierce hill tribe like that, but she had dared to do so.

"Choose!" she commanded.

Sagadar looked trapped, and he was. Whether his men would support her, she did not know. But neither did he. A slow look of resignation came over his face, and then he knelt before her.

"I will serve you," he said.

Almost, she demanded more. It was not an oath, and he might yet go back on it. It was better to take the victory that was offered though. If nothing else, it would give her time to convince him of her cause, and those with him. In the meantime, she would watch him closely.

"I accept your service," she replied. "Know also that I will serve your tribe as well. The emperor of old united many tribes into just one nation, yet he was willing to die for the protection of each one. I will be no different."

Sagadar did not seem convinced, but he said nothing. At least not in hearing of the others. Yet when she offered him her hand and he shook it, he spoke softly for her alone.

"Are the shamans so bad?"

"You would not ask that except that you know they are."

"Will you be better?"

She leaned in close. "Nothing I say will convince you if you aren't already, but look into my eyes and judge my character."

He did so, but he did not hold her gaze long. Few could. What his thoughts were though, he did not say.

"I will address your army," she said. He would not like that, but he could not go back on his word just yet. And it was best that she started this relationship as she intended it to proceed. With her in charge.

To his credit, Sagadar did not object. Both retinues returned to his army, and he addressed them for a while telling them what had transpired. Then Kubodin spoke, and for all that he seemed rough and tumble, he could speak with great eloquence when the situation demanded.

When they were done, they both bowed to her, and it was her turn to speak.

She stepped close to the front ranks so that they could see her eyes, and when they did a ripple went through them, and she heard those at the front whisper to those behind them what they had seen. Then she drew her swords and held them crosswise before her.

"I am Shar Fei," she said. "I am the heir of the emperor. Prophecy foretold me, and now destiny delivers me to you."

To her surprise, a great cheer went up at that. Yet perhaps she should have been prepared. The people were divided, just as they were over all things, but the shamans were widely hated. Most people saw through their schemes. They understood the shamans were manipulative and gathered power to themselves. They preached tolerance and righteousness, but their actions were divisive and corrupt.

"I have one goal," she proclaimed in a loud voice that carried far. "For too long the Cheng people have been held back. The tyrants have put their boots to our necks, and if we complained they pressed down harder. No more! I will sweep across the land like fire and destroy them. Where I pass, there will be battle and war. I am a warrior, but I do not like that. But I will not shrink from it. And when it is done, then just as with a fire the shoots of grass will be greener than ever before. I will lead the Cheng to victory, and even as prophecy said, even as my great forefather proclaimed when the cowardly tyrants murdered him by poison, their dark deeds will catch up to them, and I will topple them into ruin!"

The cheering started again, and they shouted her name. And in the distance Kubodin's army heard it and took up the chant also.

She looked at Sagadar, and though she said nothing to him her gaze spoke her thoughts. *Cross me if you dare, but your people will overthrow you if you do.*

She turned again to the army. "I will fight for you! If need be, I will die for you. Not for my own glory. Not to take the place of the shamans. But to free you from oppression!"

The cheering swelled, and Shar felt triumph surge within her. Even so, some warning ebbed up from a shadowy place in her mind and troubled her. She had been lucky. Fortune had favored her since Chatchek Fortress and she had gathered armies without even really trying. But good luck did not last forever. Soon, the coin would flip and she would be tested as never before.

25. Celebration

Sagadar and a large retinue stayed with Kubodin's army, while the Night Walker army returned to their own lands.

Kubodin did not waste time. Even as they marched back toward Nurthuril River where the first battle had been fought he was negotiating with the other chief. It was a good time to do so because he had just been victorious in battle. Yet he was making concessions too, and it was a good way to win an ally.

As they traveled Shar learned that the village near the battle site was Kubodin's home, and it was there that he had been born and where his father had died.

The army did not march fast, but they still reached the village before dusk. Messengers on ponies had been going back and forth, and a celebration was being prepared. It was something to look forward to, and the army sang as it walked and seemed carefree despite the turmoil and bloodshed that it had recently gone through. The hill tribes, it seemed to Shar, were resilient.

At one point Kubodin talked to a few of the mounted messengers, and he ordered that invitations be sent to all the chiefs of the hill tribes to come to his initiation as chief. It would be held in one week's time, and apparently these ceremonies were well liked and served as a great opportunity to discuss policies and trade. This was not something the Fen Wolves did with their neighboring tribes, and once more Shar realized that the grip the shamans had over the land was not as strong here.

Nevertheless, the shamans usually accompanied the chief to such ceremonies, and with Shar now revealed as heir to the emperor, and her location known, no one knew what to expect. The shamans would no doubt want to declare war on any who supported her, but would the chiefs obey that?

Whatever happened, it would be an uneasy wait, and Shar noticed that Kubodin sent scouts far and wide so that he was aware if any force approached. He would not be caught by surprise.

They came to the village and most of the army was encamped outside, but Shar, Asana and Nerchak, along with many of the leaders entered the village.

At a certain place Kubodin slowed, and Shar saw why. A hole in the ground had been dug there, and iron bars set over the top and secured into stone. She knew what it was before he spoke.

"This is the village prison," he said. "It's never used. I don't think it has been used since my grandfather's time as chief, but Kuthondrin threw me in there, and there I waited for what seemed my likely death."

Shar shivered. She could not imagine what it would be like to be placed in a pit like that, but if she were not careful the shamans would cast her into it also. Until they decided how best to kill her. That, no doubt, would be a long and torturous process carried out in public.

Asana put his arm around Kubodin's shoulders. "It's done and over now. Past wrongs have been righted, as best they can be. There's nothing left now but the future."

"You're probably right. There's one matter of the past though that still bears looking into."

He called over some of his men and gave orders for Drasta's hut to be searched for anything of interest, and for the witches who served him to be questioned as to what they knew about his father's poisoning.

"It was Kuthondrin who did it all," he said to Asana when his men had gone off to carry out his orders, "but I suspect it was Drasta who supplied the scheme and the poisons."

There was a celebration that night. Kubodin had taken the chief's hut, and others nearby had been allocated to Shar and the rest of his friends. She rested by herself for a while, unused to being alone especially in a hut. She thought of her grandmother and where she might be and what she was doing. She wondered if Shulu was even still alive, for the Ahat would be hunting her.

There were no answers to those questions though. She hoped one day to see Shulu again, but in the meantime she must do what she had been trained to do. So far, she had an army, if a very small one. Two tribes served her. It was nothing compared to the achievements of the emperor, and yet it was a start. It was more than anyone else had achieved in a thousand years.

In the face of the enmity of the shamans though, it was nothing. She would need much more than this to even have a hope of staying alive. Soon, she must turn her mind to how to make that happen. Meeting all the other clan chiefs of the Wahlum Hills when Kubodin was formally raised to the chieftainship of the Two Ravens would be a start, but she chafed at the delay. That was a week away, and her enemies would not be idle now that they knew where she was.

Dusk fell, and there was much activity outside as preparations were made for a feast. Drums began to beat, and there was something wild and primitive about them. They were not used much in the fens, but the hill tribes seemed to love them.

Shar left her hut. It, along with Kubodin's and quite a few others, formed a circle around an open area that served for such ceremonies. There were already many people collecting there, but as far as she could see such gatherings were occurring all through the village.

The drummers were stationed near the fire pits. Two trenches had been dug, and much timber had been placed in them and set alight. Later in the night, when these had died down to hot embers, the feast would be cooked on them.

She met up with Asana and then Nerchak. Kubodin came out of his hut some while later. He had not been idle but was obtaining information about all that had been happening in the tribe of late, and throughout the hills as well.

Few people spoke to Shar. Many saluted her and then scurried away, in awe of who she was. It was not a good feeling, for she enjoyed talking to strangers and seeing what they were like. The future would hold little opportunity for that. Only the nobility would talk to her, and she trusted them less. They would have ulterior motives. A warrior though, or a potter or hunter were the people she best understood. No matter the exalted blood running through her veins, that was not *her*.

At the farther edge of the light thrown by the fires, she stood a while by herself and looked into the gathering night. A fog was coming up, as it so often did here, and the stars were being swept away by it. Never had she been surrounded by so many people and felt so lonely. Like the stars themselves, she felt blotted out by powers that were beyond her. How could she dare to challenge the might of the shamans? She would die for her temerity.

She did not like the feeling of helplessness flowing over her. It was not in her nature to let a situation depress her, and again she longed for her grandmother's counsel.

Laughter and singing came from behind, and she walked back into the fire light. She found Kubodin sitting on one of the many round logs that served as chairs.

"Sit!" he said. "Battle is behind us and better days ahead."

She sat beside him, and her mood began to change but then it dropped again as men reported to Kubodin.

"We've searched Drasta's hut, chief, and questioned those who served him," one of them said. He was an older man, and no doubt once a warrior. He was of the generation of Kubodin's father, which seemed to be the type that Kubodin trusted most.

"What did you discover?"

"Two things of interest. There was a chest containing gold. Most of it was in coins, and they came from many tribes, but mostly the Nagrak Clan."

Kubodin thought on this a moment. "It was not something Drasta could have spent here. Where he got it from, and what he intended to use it for, we'll never know. No matter though. See it's distributed to the families of warriors who died in the battles. Whether they fought for me or Kuthondrin doesn't matter."

"It will be done, chief."

"And the second thing of interest?"

"We found many poisons in his hut. Some we knew, but others we couldn't identify. The witches confirmed what they were though."

Kubodin crossed his arms and kicked out the dirt with his heel. "I thought as much. Did any of them confirm Drasta supplied poison to my brother?"

"No. We questioned them hard, but they still feared to betray him even though he's dead. There was one young girl though. She hated him for some reason, and that hatred was stronger than fear. She told us that some of the gold came from Kuthondrin, but she would not, or could not, say why your brother gave it to him."

Kubodin considered that. "If she hated him, I suspect she had good reason. Give her some item of good value, and thank her. Give nothing to the rest, and send them back to their home villages. They'll not be needed here anymore."

"It will be done, chief."

"And one more thing. Make sure it becomes widely known that Drasta had a stash of gold and poisons. And that my brother paid him."

The older man nodded and walked off. He did not even salute, but Shar was learning that the hill tribes were not keen on formality. Kubodin himself was a perfect example of what they were like, and the little man had not even noticed.

The drums picked up a different beat now, and many of the crowd danced. Those who did not were drinking a strong ale. Shar was given some, but she found it harsh and only sipped at it.

"Better than nahaz," Kubodin said with a wink.

Shar thought back to their brief venture on the Nagrak plains, and the tribesman they had met there. It was not so long ago, but so much had happened since then that it seemed an event from the deep past.

A man came to Kubodin with a message, and Kubodin nodded. Shar had not caught what the man had said, but it soon became clear. A group of warriors, their hands tied were brought to stand before their new chief. They were the nazram who had formed Drasta's guard in the battle. They did not look happy, and Shar did not blame them. It was well known how much Kubodin hated them, for it was their kind who had pursued, tortured and nearly killed him years ago.

"Do any of you deny being Drasta's nazram?" Kubodin asked.

No one answered.

"Will you forsake all ties with the shamans?"

Again, there was no answer. Kubodin thought a few moments, and his face was dark. Shar had a bad feeling, and pity welled in her for these men. Was it their fault that the shamans were as they were? Could they be blamed for following a path that rewarded them with a better life?

Kubodin was stern though. "Then by your actions you have earned death. Give me a reason why it should not be so."

Again, there was silence, but into that Shar spoke. "The people are not the enemy. The shamans sit in the center of power like a spider in its web. They are the evil that poisons the land. Kubodin, my friend, will you spare the lives of these men for me? I will accept their service, if they are willing to give it."

Kubodin fingered his axe, and his eyes still looked dark. Nor did he reply straight away.

"You are more lenient than I," he said eventually.

The nazram stood proud and tall, and they seemed to Shar like men who were prepared to die. If nothing else, they had courage. And men such as that would be needed in the days ahead.

"More lenient, perhaps. But no lesser taskmaster than the shamans." She stood, and drew her twin blades. "These are the Swords of Dawn and Dusk. This is a triseptium year, and all things are possible in it, for fate charges every minute. Most of all, I am the heir to the emperor. All your old allegiances are as dust, but the new land that is waiting, the future Cheng Empire that will be, needs men such as you. If you swear loyalty to me, touching the hands that hold the blades, I will walk with you into that future."

Kubodin had not quite agreed to spare them yet, and she was usurping his authority. He was chief, and these were his tribesmen. Yet he had pledged to serve her as emperor, and it was best to put that to the test early. Moreover, and she hoped he understood this, war was coming. If she showed mercy and allowed men who had been enemies to join her it would set an example for the future. If enemies knew that defeat meant death, they would only fight all the harder.

26. Cold Steel

The nazram hesitated, and Kubodin scowled. "Dogs! The emperor has offered you mercy and a prosperous future. It's better than the death I would have given you!"

Shar was not so sure about either of those things. Anyone tied to her faced the wrath of the shamans. And Kubodin might not have killed the nazram. He might have brought this whole situation about in order for her to do exactly as she had done and strengthen her authority. He might be simplistic in appearance, but his was a sharp mind capable of such a scheme, and a lot more.

One of the nazram stood before her, and reluctantly he clasped her hands, being very careful not to touch the blades, and swore obedience to her.

The others, one by one, followed his example. They still seemed sullen, but Shar saw hope in a few eyes, and she vowed to herself that she would treat all who came to her in the future such as this. Enemies would have their past sins forgiven if they vowed to serve the future empire. Some would no doubt try to betray her if the situation allowed for it, but some at least would be genuine.

"Know that from this moment on," Kubodin proclaimed, "there are no nazram in the Two Ravens Clan." He looked coldly at those who once had held that title. "But the emperor has freed you from your past, and you are warriors now of the tribe. Go in peace, and earn back the favor she has given you."

The men bowed, though not to him. They offered their respect to her, and then left.

Kubodin grinned. "Nicely done," he said, speaking quietly.

Shar knew then that her earlier suspicion was correct, and he had contrived this situation.

The night wore on, and they feasted. The strong ale became more palatable to Shar, and she drank too much. By midnight she was unsteady on her feet and cursed herself. She was not used to drinking, and she had made herself vulnerable. Kubodin, who drank half a dozen cups to her one, seemed unchanged.

She left, circling the feasting area and trying to get some fresh air and steady herself, and then retired to her hut. Two warriors stood without it. Kubodin had told her that he would give her guards, and she was glad of it. She would have enemies out there who would do her harm, for despite all the celebrations there were no doubt some who hated her and loved the shamans. She greeted them warmly, for they would be men Kubodin trusted greatly, and they saluted her in turn.

Sleep did not come quickly. But it seemed the celebration ended not long after she had gone herself, for the drums were still now and there was no noise from outside.

Shar slept, then woke, then slept again and dreamed. And it was not a pleasant dream. Her fear was what the shamans would do to her if they defeated her, and that infused her sleep.

She looked up from the pit in which Kubodin had been imprisoned, and shamans leered down at her through the iron bars. Then she was in a cage on a wagon, and she knew where she was being taken to. Three Moon Mountain was the stronghold of the shamans, and it was said that none but shamans ever ventured inside. Except those they questioned, and those unfortunate souls never came back to the world they had left.

The mountain drew closer, and now it seemed like a terrible giant of a man with a head and two shoulders, and he reached out to crush her.

Shar woke with a scream on her lips, but she stifled it. A cold sweat bathed her, and her heart fluttered wildly in her chest. She lay back on the thick bearskin that formed her bed, frightened and confused, and it seemed to her that even in the pitch-black night of the hut there was a shadow in the room. It loomed over her, and she recognized it.

It was the ghostly figure that had saved her and the others from the nazram at the coastal village.

"Awake! Awake!" it cried, but the fog of sleep was still on Shar, and she struggled to move and grasp her swords that lay on the floor nearby.

Then there was another shadow, and something crashed into the side of her head with great force. Pain roared through her, and then consciousness faded.

She woke, unsure how much time had passed. Not much, she thought. Pain still throbbed through the whole side of her head and she felt sick. There was blood too. It ran down her face and onto her neck. She tried to call out, but found that she had been gagged. Her hands were free though, but even as she moved them the cold touch of steel rested against her throat.

"Move, and you die," came a whisper in her ear. She knew that voice, but it sounded different from before.

"We're going somewhere," the voice said. "Put on your boots. And strap on your swords. We're not leaving those little trinkets behind."

Shar struggled upward. She fumbled for her boots and tried to think. She could not believe this was happening, but whether it was the ale or the blow to her head she was confused. All she knew was that she wanted to escape, but the knife was held firm against her throat. To move the wrong way was to have her lifeblood spilled onto the floor of the hut.

When she was ready, the voice whispered in her ear again.

"Tie your hands together."

She felt a length of thin rope fall over her shoulder, and she grasped it. Nearly, she attacked, for once her hands were tied she would lose practically all ability to try to get herself out of this situation. But she could not. The knife was hard against her throat, and her enemy behind her. To do anything but obey was to die.

The rope had a knot already tied in it, and she did as asked and slipped her hands through and tightened it. When she was done, his other hand slipped around from behind her and tightened it more, all the while the knife pressed harder against her throat until she felt it cut the skin.

"Now move, *princess*," the voice whispered sarcastically. "Out the door and northward away from this accursed village. If you try to run, I'll kill you. If you make a sound, I'll kill you. If you so much as turn your head the wrong way, I'll slice your throat and gut you like a pig. Do you understand?"

Shar felt rage boil up inside her, but she nodded her head.

They moved out of the hut then, her deadly shadow always behind her, the cold steel never relenting. Outside the hut her anger flared even higher, for the two guards stationed there were dead. Their limp forms were hard to see in the dark, but she could make them out. They had died protecting her, and their death was on her conscience. Had they been anywhere else in the world beside near to her, they would both still be alive.

Like shadows, Shar and her abductor passed through the village. She wanted to scream or to run, but she could do neither. She did manage to tread hard in a few places hoping to leave tracks that could be followed, but it was probably futile in a village where so many people would obscure any trail she left as soon as dawn came.

Dawn was hours away too, and the dark of the night crept into her soul. At whiles her anger towered high, then it collapsed into despair. At other times fear took hold of her body, and she trembled.

"Turn a little to the left, princess."

She hated that voice. It reminded her of her own stupidity, for she had been betrayed and walked openly into this situation. Yet she obeyed, and she ground her teeth in futile rage that she had no choice but to do so.

They were out of the village now and into the farmland that surrounded it. Was he going to kill her here? She could be sure of nothing, but she did not think so. Not yet. It would have been easier to do so in the hut.

She discovered why he was leading her here quickly. There was a corral, and in it she could vaguely see the dark shapes of ponies as they grazed in the night. This was where the messengers kept their horses.

Unexpectedly, her arm was grabbed and she felt a sharp pain as a finger thrust deep into her flesh against a pressure point. At the same moment her captor used the thumb of the hand that held the knife to strike the corresponding one in her neck. Darkness swamped her. She fought it, but the art of dar shun was a skilled one, and her captor had used it well. The next blow that struck her on the back of the head was less skilled. It was not dar shun, but merely a brutal blow. Yet it was too much for her, and the darkness won.

When she woke it was dawn. She was stiff and sore all over, and she felt completely disorientated. The ground seemed to move beneath her, and she nearly vomited. She held herself in check though, and fought back the despair and fear that washed over her in a wave.

She must think. She must be calm. She must not give in to panic.

Quickly she realized what had happened. Her feet were bound together now, and she was thrown over the saddle of a pony on her stomach and tied down. Like a sack she was being carted wherever her captor took her, and anger rose in her again.

It did not last long. Her position was uncomfortable, and pain grew swiftly. Her hands were worse though. When she was unconscious her captor had tightened the rope that held them, and it cut into her skin with a raw pain that made her want to scream.

She made no sound though. She would not give that satisfaction to her enemy. She tried as best she could to raise her head so she could see better, but her neck ached at that. She did catch a glimpse of the countryside though. They were out of the valley where her friends and any chance of rescue lay, and it was miles behind them.

The dead guards would have been discovered. Her absence would now be known. If anyone chose to search for her though, where would they look? The hills were vast, and tracking her where so many others had trod would be impossible. The theft of the pony would be a clue, but no doubt her captor had thought of that. He would have released all the other ponies and scattered them so that their tracks were everywhere and in all directions.

She heard the steady gait of his own pony ahead of her, no doubt leading hers by a rope. She could not see him, but she pictured his face and she hated him.

For now, there was nothing to do. She tried to relax into the pain that wracked her body, and to ignore it. So she had been taught to do, and she had learned that skill.

But this was different. This was not the sharp blow of a punch to her face that was there and then receded. It was continued and enduring. It did not relent, but rather grew worse.

She tried to distract herself from the pain, and there was one question that rose to the front of her mind and demanded an answer. Who, or what, was the figure that had tried to warn her?

It had saved them before. And it had tried to save her last night, only she had woken too slowly to defend herself. That it was friendly to her, there was no doubt. Likewise, there was no doubt that it was a creature of magic rather than flesh and blood.

Could it be a ghost? She could not discount that. She had seen some strange things on this journey. She did not really believe it though. If not a ghost though, then what?

The pony came to a stop, and a few moments later she heard the footsteps of her captor approach. He came to the side of the pony where her head rested, but she was too tired to try to lift her head up to see what he was doing.

"I'll rest here a little while, princess. No one lives near here that I can see, and certainly no one will find us, but you can stay tied and gagged just as you are."

He sat down and ate something a little distance away, but he offered her nothing. Food did not matter at the moment, but she had a raging thirst. She would not try to communicate that to him though. He must already know that she would be thirsty, and she would not give him the satisfaction of asking for anything.

When he was done, he approached and spoke to her again.

"The backward scum in these hills might think of you as some sort of princess, but you know better now, don't you?"

She gave no answer, and he roughly pulled her head up by her hair so she could see him, and he loosed the gag so that she could speak.

"Answer me!"

Pain and humiliation roared through her. She tried to answer, but her mouth was dry and she struggled to breathe in the position he held her.

"Why?" she croaked.

His face was as it always had been, but now she realized that boy as he seemed to be, he had hidden his true feelings beneath a perfect mask.

He sneered at her. "Why? Because you're money to me. When I bring you in you'll make me rich. You have no idea how I longed to capture you before now, but I'm a patient man and waited until I could ensure no one would be able to follow us." He laughed, and it was so like his normal laugh but now she heard some shadow of cruelty in it that she had not before.

"You still don't know who I am, do you?"

"I trusted you, Nerchak."

"Nerchak? That's not my name. If you want to know who I am, this will tell you all."

He raised his arm then, and allowed the sleeve to fall down toward his elbow. Tattooed on the skin was a black serpent, winding its way down toward his wrist where it spat crimson venom. It was the sign of the Ahat. It was the mark of an assassin, and shock filled her veins like ice.

He reefed the gag back into her mouth and slapped her hard for no reason other than he could.

"You're mine now, princess. I'm going to sell you for money, but if you give me any trouble I'll settle for the glory of being the one to kill you. Remember that, and you might live a little while longer."

She did not see him go, but she heard his footsteps and then her pony started to move again. Tears ran down her face, and blood as well, for his blow had caused the wound in her head from last night to bleed again.

If she had not plumbed the depths of despair before, she did so now. She was helpless in the hands of a skilled enemy, and he was going to sell her to the shamans who would gladly pay a fortune to be the ones to kill her themselves.

Thus ends *Swords of Wizardry*. The Shaman's Sword series continues in book three, *Swords of Defiance*, where Shar will discover if the prophecy of her great forefather is strong enough to contend with evil, and if she has the courage to be its instrument…

SWORDS OF DEFIANCE

BOOK THREE OF THE SHAMAN'S SWORD SERIES

COMING SOON!

Amazon lists millions of titles, and I'm glad you discovered this one. But if you'd like to know when I release a new book, instead of leaving it to chance, sign up for my new release list. I'll send you an email on publication.

Yes please! – Go to www.homeofhighfantasy.com and sign up.

No thanks – I'll take my chances.

Dedication

There's a growing movement in fantasy literature. Its name is noblebright, and it's the opposite of grimdark.

Noblebright celebrates the virtues of heroism. It's an old-fashioned thing, as old as the first story ever told around a smoky campfire beneath ancient stars. It's storytelling that highlights courage and loyalty and hope for the spirit of humanity. It recognizes the dark, the dark in us all, and the dark in the villains of its stories. It recognizes death, and treachery and betrayal. But it dwells on none of these things.

I dedicate this book, such as it is, to that which is noblebright. And I thank the authors before me who held the torch high so that I could see the path: J.R.R. Tolkien, C.S. Lewis, Terry Brooks, Susan Cooper, Roger Taylor and many others. I salute you.

And, for a time, I too shall hold the torch high.

Appendix: Encyclopedic Glossary

Note: The history of the Cheng Empire is obscure, for the shamans hid much of it. Yet the truth was recorded in many places and passed down in family histories, in secret societies and especially among warrior culture. This glossary draws on much of that 'secret' history, and each book in this series is individualized to reflect the personal accounts that have come down through the dark tracts of time to the main actors within each book's pages. Additionally, there is often historical material provided in its entries for people, artifacts and events that are not included in the main text.

Many races dwell in Alithoras. All have their own language, and though sometimes related to one another the changes sparked by migration, isolation and various influences often render these tongues unintelligible to each other.

The ascendancy of Halathrin culture across the land, who are sometimes called elves, combined with their widespread efforts to secure and maintain allies against various evil incursions, has made their language the primary means of communication between diverse peoples. This was especially so during the Shadowed Wars, but has persisted through the centuries afterward.

This glossary contains a range of names and terms. Some are of Halathrin origin, and their meaning is provided.

The Cheng culture is also revered by its people, and many names are given in their tongue. It is important to remember that the empire was vast though, and there is no one Cheng language but rather a multitude of dialects. Perfect consistency of spelling and meaning is therefore not to be looked for.

List of abbreviations:

Cam. Camar

Chg. Cheng

Comb. Combined

Cor. Corrupted form

Hal. Halathrin

Prn. Pronounced

Ahat: *Chg.* "Hawk in the night." A special kind of assassin. Used by the shamans in particular, but open for hire to anybody who can afford their fee. It is said that the shamans subverted an entire tribe in the distant past, and that every member of the community, from the children to the elderly, train to hone their craft at killing and nothing else. They grow no crops, raise no livestock nor pursue any trade save the bringing of death. The fees of their assignments pay for all their needs. This is legend only, for no such community has ever been found. But the lands of the Cheng are wide and such a community, if it exists, would be hidden and guarded.

Antrathadaba: Etymology unknown, though certainly not a word of Cheng origin. It is an ancient city, now almost buried by time.

Asana: *Chg.* "Gift of light." Rumored to be the greatest swordmaster in the history of the Cheng people. His father was a Duthenor tribesman from outside the bounds of the old Cheng Empire.

Bald Hill: An ancient hill fort in Two Ravens territory. Legend claims it was constructed by the elves in a time before the Cheng dwelt in the land.

Chatchek Fortress: *Chg.* "Hollow mountain." An ancient fortress once conquered by Chen Fei. It predates the Cheng Empire however, having been constructed two thousand years prior to that time. It is said it was established to protect a trade route where gold was mined and transported to the surrounding lands.

Chen Fei: *Chg.* "Graceful swan." Swans are considered birds of wisdom and elegance in Cheng culture. It is said that one flew overhead at the time of Chen's birth, and his mother named him for it. He rose from poverty to become emperor of his people, and he was loved by many but despised by some. He was warrior, general, husband, father, poet, philosopher, painter, but most of all he was enemy to the machinations of the shamans who tried to secretly govern all aspects of the people.

Cheng: *Chg.* "Warrior." The overall name of the various related tribes united by Chen Fei. It was a word for warrior in his dialect, later adopted for his growing army and last of all for the people of his nation. His empire disintegrated after his assassination, but much of the culture he fostered endured.

Cheng Empire: A vast array of realms formerly governed by kings and united, briefly, under Chen Fei. One of the largest empires ever to rise in Alithoras.

Dar shun: *Chg.* "The points that vibrate." The art of using the pressure points of the human body to heal, harm or kill. A secret skill passed down in elite warrior and healer societies. Its knowledge and workings are revered, and only handed down to students of high moral character. Except for the Ahat. But even among them it is taught to few.

Drasta: *Chg.* "Ice." Shaman of the Two Ravens Clan.

Drugu: *Chg.* "Dark secret." A senior shaman with authority over the Nagrak Tribe.

Eagle Claw Mountains: A mountain range toward the south of the Cheng Empire. It is said the people who later became the Cheng lived here first and over centuries moved out to populate the surrounding lands. Others believe that these people were blue-eyed, and intermixed with various other races as they came down off the mountains to trade and make war.

Elves: See Halathrin.

Elù-haraken: *Hal.* "The shadowed wars." Long ago battles in a time that is become myth to the Cheng tribes.

Fen Wolf Tribe: A tribe that live in Tsarin Fen. Once, they and the neighboring Soaring Eagle Tribe were one people and part of a kingdom. It is also told that Chen Fei was born in that realm.

Fields of Rah: Rah signifies "ocean of the sky" in many Cheng dialects. It is a country of vast grasslands but at its center is Nagrak City, which of old was the capital of the empire. It was in this city that the emperor was assassinated.

Gan: *Chg.* "They who have attained." It is an honorary title added to a person's name after they have acquired great skill. It can be applied to warriors, shamans, sculptors, weavers or any particular expertise. It is reserved for the greatest of the best.

Halathrin: *Hal.* "People of Halath." A race of elves named after an honored lord who led an exodus of his people to the land of Alithoras in pursuit of justice, having sworn to defeat a great evil. They are human, though of fairer form, greater skill and higher culture. They possess a unity of body, mind and spirit that enables insight and endurance beyond the native races of Alithoras. Said to be immortal, but killed in great numbers during their conflicts in ancient times with the evil they sought to destroy. Those conflicts are collectively known as the Shadowed Wars.

Halls of Lore: Essentially, a library within the stronghold of the lòhrens in northern Alithoras. It serves as a repository for the known history of humanity and the wisdom of the ages.

Harakness: *Chg.* "The tears of the earth." The Cheng god of water.

Harledrek: *Chg.* "Keeper of the Gate." The goddess of death. Often depicted as snake headed. Some clans deem her evil, while others see her as a necessary force of order in the universe. Her twin sister is the goddess of life.

Heart of the Hurricane: The shaman's term for the state of mind warriors call Stillness in the Storm. See that term for further information.

Iron Dog Clan: A tribe of the Wahlum Hills. So named for their legendary endurance and determination.

Kubodin: *Chg.* Etymology unknown. A wild warrior from the Wahlum Hills. Simple appearing, but far more than he seems. Asana's manservant and friend.

Kuthondrin: *Chg.* Etymology unknown. Brother to Kubodin.

Lòhren: *Hal. Prn.* Ler-ren. "Knowledge giver – a counselor." Other terms used by various nations include sage, wizard, and druid.

Magic: Mystic power.

Nagadar Village: The head village of the Two Ravens Clan. Named after an ancient hero.

Nahaz: *Chg.* "White fire." A spirit fermented from mare's milk. Originated in the Nagrak Tribe, but traded throughout the tribes. Said to possess recuperative powers, and used in many rituals.

Nagrak: *Chg.* "Those who follow the herds." A Cheng tribe that dwell on the Fields of Rah. Traditionally they lived a nomadic lifestyle, traveling in the wake of herds of wild cattle that provided all their needs. But an element of their tribe, and some contend this was another tribe in origin that they conquered, are great builders and live in a city.

Nagrak City: A city at the heart of the Fields of Rah. Once the capital of the Cheng Empire.

Namarlin: *Chg.* "Morning mist." A warrior and trusted friend of Kubodin's father.

Namaya: *Chg.* "Morning radiance." An alias used by Shar.

Nazram: *Chg.* "The wheat grains that are prized after the chaff is excluded." An elite warrior organization that is in service to the shamans. For the most part, they are selected from those who quest for the twin swords each triseptium, though there are exceptions to this.

Nerchak: *Chg.* "Hollow tooth." A young man who befriends Shar. His name is also a term for jewelry made from the teeth, horns or tusks of dangerous animals that are strung into a necklace or bracelet. In some dialects, the word is spelled "nerchek" and is a euphemism for venomous snakes.

Night Walker Clan: A tribe of the Wahlum Hills. The name derives from their totem animal, which is a nocturnal predator of thick forests. It's a type of cat, small but fierce and covered in black fur.

Nomochek: *Chg.* "Hollow tree – bamboo." A warrior of the Two Ravens Clan.

Nurthuril: Etymology unknown, though suspected to be a word of Halathrin origin. A river in the Wahlum Hills.

Olekhai: *Chg.* "The falcon that plummets." A famous and often used name in the old world before, and during, the Cheng Empire. Never used since the assassination of the emperor, however. The most prominent bearer of the name during the days of the emperor was the chief of his council of wise men. He was, essentially, prime minister of the emperor's government. But he betrayed his lord and his people. Shulu Gan spared his life, but only so as to punish him with a terrible curse.

Quest of Swords: Occurs every triseptium to mark the three times seven years the shamans lived in exile during the emperor's life. The best warriors of each clan seek the twin swords of the emperor. Used by the shamans as a means of finding the most skilled warriors in the land and recruiting them to their service.

Radatan: *Chg.* "The ears that flick – a slang term for deer." A hunter of the Two Ravens Clan.

Running Bear Clan: A tribe of the Wahlum Hills. Their totem is a species of small bear that inhabits the hills.

Sagadar: *Chg.* "Willow tree." Chief of the Night Walker Clan.

Shadowed Wars: See Elù-haraken.

Shapechanger: Prominent figures in Cheng legend and history. They are beings able to take any form, and are renowned for being mischievous. Other stories, or histories, claim they are creatures of evil in servitude to the shamans.

Shaman: The religious leaders of the Cheng people. They are sorcerers, and though the empire is fragmented they work as one across the lands to serve their own united purpose. Their spiritual home is Three Moon Mountain, but few save shamans have ever been there.

Shar: *Chg.* "White stone – the peak of a mountain." A young woman of the Fen Wolf tribe. Claimed by Shulu Gan to be the descendent of Chen Fei.

Shulu Gan: *Chg.* The first element signifies "magpie". A name given to the then leader of the shamans for her hair was black, save for a streak of white that ran through it.

Shunwahrin: *Chg.* "The mist that crowns a hill." Leader of the Two Ravens nazram.

Skultic Mountains: *Chg.* "Rocks of doom." Mountain range in the southwest of the old empire of the Cheng. Abandoned, often claimed to be haunted, and a barren landscape. Most likely the lack of fertile ground is the main reason no one lives there.

Smoking Eyes Clan: A tribe of the Wahlum Hills. Named for a god, who they take as their totem.

Soaring Eagle Tribe: A tribe that borders the Fen Wolf clan. At one time, one with them, but now, as is the situation with most tribes, hostilities are common. The eagle is their totem, for the birds are plentiful in the mountain lands to the south and often soar far from their preferred habitat over the tribe's grasslands.

Stillness in the Storm: The state of mind a true warrior seeks in battle. Neither angry nor scared, neither hopeful nor worried. When emotion is banished from the mind, the body is free to express the skill acquired through long years of training. Sometimes also called Calmness in the Storm or the Heart of the Hurricane.

Swimming Osprey Clan: A tribe of the Wahlum Hills. Their totem is the osprey, often seen diving into the ocean to catch fish.

Taga Nashu: *Chg.* "The Grandmother who does not die." One of the many epithets of Shulu Gan, greatest of the shamans but cast from their order.

Three Moon Mountain: A mountain in the Eagle Claw range. Famed as the home of the shamans. None know what the three moons reference relates to except, perhaps, the shamans.

Triseptium: A period of three times seven years. It signifies the exiles of the shamans during the life of the emperor. Declared by the shamans as a cultural treasure, and celebrated by them. Less so by the tribes, but the shamans encourage it. Much more popular now than in past ages.

Tsarin Fen: *Chg.* Tsarin, which signifies mountain cat, was a general under Chen Fei. It is said he retired to the swamp after the death of his leader. At one time, many regions and villages were named after generals, but the shamans changed the names and did all they could to make people forget the old ones. In their view, all who served the emperor were criminals and their achievements were not to be celebrated. Tsarin Fen is one of the few such names that still survive.

Tsergar: *Chg.* "Spear fish." Formerly a nazram, but now a ship's captain.

Tsogodin: *Chg.* "The clamor of distant battle." A warrior of the Two Ravens Clan.

Two Ravens Clan: A tribe of the Wahlum Hills. Their totem is the raven.

Wahlum Hills: *Chg. Comb. Hal.* "Mist-shrouded highlands." Hills to the north-west of the old Cheng empire, and home to Kubodin.

About the author

I'm a man born in the wrong era. My heart yearns for faraway places and even further afield times. Tolkien had me at the beginning of *The Hobbit* when he said, ". . . one morning long ago in the quiet of the world . . ."

Sometimes I imagine myself in a Viking mead-hall. The long winter night presses in, but the shimmering embers of a log in the hearth hold back both cold and dark. The chieftain calls for a story, and I take a sip from my drinking horn and stand up . . .

Or maybe the desert stars shine bright and clear, obscured occasionally by wisps of smoke from burning camel dung. A dry gust of wind marches sand grains across our lonely campsite, and the wayfarers about me stir restlessly. I sip cool water and begin to speak.

I'm a storyteller. A man to paint a picture by the slow music of words. I like to bring faraway places and times to life, to make hearts yearn for something they can never have, unless for a passing moment.

Made in the USA
Monee, IL
10 July 2024